Night Flight

GERALD HAUSMAN

PHILOMEL BOOKS

NEW YORK

Copyright © 1996 by Gerald Hausman.   All rights reserved.
This book, or parts thereof, may not be reproduced in any form without
permission in writing from the publisher, Philomel Books, a division of
The Putnam & Grosset Group, 200 Madison Avenue, New York, NY 10016.
Philomel Books, Reg. U.S. Pat. & Tm. Off. Published simultaneously in Canada.
Book design by Gunta Alexander. The text is set in Janson.
Library of Congress Cataloging-in-Publication Data
Hausman, Gerald.   Night flight / Gerald Hausman. p. cm.
Summary: During the summer of 1957 when both their dogs are poisoned,
twelve-year-old Jeff must come to terms with his own Jewish identity and
with his best friend's brutality and prejudice.
1. Jews—United States—Juvenile fiction.[1. Jews—United States—Fiction.
2. Prejudices—Fiction.3. Friendship—Fiction.] I. Title.   PZ7.H2883Ni
1996 [Fic]—dc20   95-156 CIP   AC   ISBN 0-399-22758-X
10 9 8 7 6 5 4 3 2 1   First Impression

For Pat Gauch, who spent long hours
looking under leaves with one who tried to,
but could not, forget. —G.H.

Contents

Prologue

We used to sit up in the crow's nest, a hunter's blind built by my grandfather back in the thirties, and watch what happened on the lake. It was like sitting on our own private cloud; we could see without being seen, and we could hear without being heard.

We liked to look out into the swamp and see the herons that nested there. And watch, at dawn, a family of raccoons wash their breakfast of crayfish on the beach. One morning we saw the old man of the swamp, the great snapping turtle. We both knew the legend, how the old turtle had saved a Mahican girl from drowning; how he had taken her on his round, mossy back and brought her to shore.

So began that year on the lake, a summer, we thought, like all the rest. Little did we realize that the world as we knew it would be changed forever. It started one misty night on the crow's nest the summer of nineteen fifty-seven.

1 · Crow's Nest

My grandfather's lookout was built between four great pines that grew on the bluff overlooking the lake. When the wind blew, the pines sighed and the crow's nest leaned out over the lake. No place, except maybe the gorge by Max's house, had more magic than this old hunter's blind that creaked in the wind. Here we hunted the woods and haunted the beach, rifles in hand; something we had done for as many years as I could remember.

We were camping that night, waiting to see a family of flying squirrels that lived in a hollow, lightning-struck tree across from the crow's nest. Our dogs, Silver and Tony, were playing in the moonlight, down by the beach. We never went anywhere without them. The night was loud with frogs, bright with stars. A perfect night.

"How do you know we're going to see the flying squirrels?" I asked Max.

"I just know," he said. He was taking deep breaths, blowing up his air mattress, *phitt-phitt-phitt.*

Max, the old pro, was twelve, just like I was, but somehow the way he acted seemed much older to me. I watched him now, keeping an eye, as well, on the hollow, bark-stripped tree. From where I stood I could see across the lake to the town lights of Oak Wood, where the immigrant families lived. And, looking in the other direction, I could see the church steeple, white and sharp, from the nearby town of Deserted Village, where Max and his parents had their house. Our place, just down from the crow's nest, was on the only peninsula that went out into the lake.

"Do you think Silver and Tony are going to scare the squirrels?" I asked Max.

In the moonlight, his red hair was white, his face made of marble. He stopped puffing on his mattress and looked at me sullenly.

"If you're so nervous about it, why don't you go down there and quiet them?" That was the thing about Max; he always had the answers. Always.

I climbed down the ladder. The dogs had gone over toward the swamp by the Fensters' icehouse. They were the old couple, our closest neighbors, who made their living sawing ice out of the lake and selling it in the summer. They had a big barn they stored it in.

I went down the moon-filled path, parted the ferns at the bottom, and headed into the swamp. The two dogs, who were as inseparable as Max and me, were barking at something close by.

Peering into the broken-tooth forest of swamp pines, I saw

what looked like a bunch of black-and-white rowboats teth-
ered to the cattails. The dogs were barking near there. I took
a few more steps in that direction. There came, then, a
strange squooshing and snorting, and the boats moved a little,
drifted nearer.

I stopped walking. Up in the crow's nest, I could hear Max
puffing at his mattress. The dogs kept barking. The spotted
boats drifted closer. Digging my hand in my pocket, I
plucked out my flashlight, snapped on the beam, and directed
it at the swamp boats.

They blinked, proving to be a couple of stray cows with
waterweeds hanging out of their mouths. I flicked off my
light, laughed. Then I called Silver and Tony. They came
out of the ferny brush, splashing and chasing each other.

"What's going on?" Max asked when I got back to the ladder. He was waiting for me on the ground.

"The dogs were trying to tree a couple of cows," I told
him.

He chuckled, and called Tony. The big golden retriever
jumped up and put his great paws on Max's shoulders. In the
moonlight, Silver's glistening coat was living up to her name.
She smelled swampy, but I gave her a hug just the same.

After we fed Silver and Tony, they stretched out at the
foot of the crow's nest, side by side. They'd known each other
since they were pups, and they loved our camp-outs. We let
them run free as much as they wanted, and they'd come back
to camp with their tongues hanging out, fur coated with mud.
Soon the dogs were both asleep, their paws dancing in sepa-

rate dreams. I wondered what it was that made them whimper in those tiny voices of birdlike alarm.

"They're okay now," Max said. "Let's climb back up so we can watch the squirrels. It's almost time."

"How can you be so sure we're going to see any?" I asked, ascending the ladder.

"I can feel it," Max insisted, "right here."

He tapped his heart.

Somehow, Max, the hunter, always knew what was coming. He had the instinct of an animal and the mind of a man. We were bathed in cloud-light. The woods lay white as snow. The silence was thick as cotton. Then there came a scratching sound. Max was at the railing, pointing.

2 · Flying Squirrel

I saw the little round head of one pop out of the hollow tree.

"That's the male," Max whispered.

"How do you know?"

"They're bigger, see? The female's already out on the limb."

Now I could see both of them. They were nearly level with us and, perhaps because of that reason, they didn't pay us any attention. The flying squirrels had huge, black marble eyes. They were grayish brown from head to tail, but their undersides were white.

Hopping delicately along the limb, they touched noses, then the bolder one dived into the empty air.

I felt my heart stop. He made a great, breathtaking moon-leap and landed some twenty yards away on the side of a tree. Then his sleek little companion followed him, riding on the air like an acrobat, gliding on silky strands of invisible moon-light.

I couldn't believe our luck—to see such a magic moment!

"Told you so." Max nodded in that cool, superior way of his. "Told you we'd see them."

I nodded, pleased. He'd shown me a fisher's nest once, and nobody but Max knew how to collect red efts, those pretty orange salamanders with the crimson spots on their backs. He had a knack, all right, when it came to seeing things in the woods. He had a knack for a lot of things.

Then, suddenly, the bright night darkened.

"Did you hear that?" Max asked.

It sounded like someone screaming.

We peered into the trees.

Then came a hideous volley of squabbles and yells, the most unimaginable sounds you ever heard—chuckles, barks, hisses, all kinds of shrieks. It was a language of demons, and very close by. The flying squirrels froze on a pine bough.

Uh-huh-wee-ay-huhk, came the weird voice of the woods.

"You know what that is?" Max asked, grinning.

I shook my head.

"It's a barred owl." He gestured to a limb on another dead tree not twenty yards away. A large-eyed owl was sitting there. *Uh-huh-wee-ay-huhk*, it hissed and coughed again, sounding almost, but not quite, human.

Then it dropped soundlessly, traveling through the air, sweeping down, claws extended. We watched, horrified, as the smaller squirrel panicked and took flight before the dark-winged shadow. Without a sound, the hunter caught the squirrel on the wing and flew off into the ghostly trees. It was over almost before it began. Silver and Tony were barking like crazy, and we climbed down to quiet them.

"Did you see how the owl caught that squirrel?" Max asked as he patted Tony. "Wasn't that the coolest thing you ever saw?"

I looked at him in the shadows. "Yeah," I answered. I felt empty. Silver growled, staring in the direction of the owl. The moon rode higher in the sky; it came over the crow's nest and brightened the dark hills in back of the swamp.

After a while, when the dogs lay down, we climbed back up and got into our sleeping bags, but when I closed my eyes, I saw the talons open and shut, the squirrel taken, the owl float out into the night. Max was already asleep, snoring. But I kept seeing the hooked claws, the smoky feathers, the night flight. Finally, though, I began to get drowsy and, at last, fell asleep and dreamed.

I was a flying squirrel, gliding over the lake. Flying over fog-haired Fensters and their ice barn. Beyond the swamp to the north, where the peaked roofs of Oak Wood rose above the fortress oaks. And then I was soaring to the south, where the close-set colonial houses of Deserted Village were gathered. There was Max's house, like an old white clipper ship in a sea of roses. And there, as I flew by, was Max himself. He walked through the wheat-colored grass in tall, black rubber boots, rifle in one hand, brown burlap bag in the other. The bag was moving, as if something were inside it.

3 · Lake Burial

I sat up, surprised to find myself on the crow's nest. Max was still asleep. I crept out of my sleeping bag and looked at the hollow tree. The night was unchanged but for a strange coughing sound. The owl? Back again to capture the other squirrel? I stared into the moonlit woods, the pines so straight and dark.

I moved over to the side. The cough was louder there, but more like a choking noise now. Then I saw Silver, clawing the earth, trying to stand. Her face was flecked with foam—not moon this time, but something else.

I woke Max and then I climbed down the ladder. "Foaming at the mouth means rabies," he mumbled, hesitating above me on the ladder. I ignored him and jumped off.

"Get back," he warned. I knelt at Silver's side. Her lovely crow's-wing coat was covered with foam. She looked up at me, her tail thumped twice.

"Silver," I said, "what's the matter, girl?" I'd had her since I was seven, and she'd never been sick once.

I stroked her head. Max whispered "rabies" from the ladder. Then Silver sucked a raspy breath. It didn't make sense. She had been fine an hour before. Struggling to get air, she pawed to get up. I tried to help her, but she fell back heavily. Then she started sucking air again, her eyes wild with alarm. I put my head on her chest and heard her distant heartbeat like a far-off bell. "Don't die," I whispered, "please don't die."

But as I knelt at her side, Silver closed her eyes and sighed so deeply that I felt my own breath escape me. There came one last choked breath, and then my beautiful Belgian shepherd was dead. I heard Max calling out for Tony, but dimly, as if he called from another world. I just lay there with my dog. Maybe I was waiting for her to breathe again, even though I knew she wouldn't.

"I'm going to bring Silver home," I said at last, fighting back the tears. Her head hung loosely as I took her in my arms, bearing her weight breathlessly down through the ferns at the bottom of the grove. As I walked along, I thought it was impossible. How could I be carrying Silver, who was alive just a few minutes ago? How could she be dead? The silent owl shot through my mind as the gray light gave way to red dawn. I had to set Silver down and rest before going on. I could hear Max calling out for Tony from the hill by the crow's nest.

My mom was up, moving around in the kitchen when I came in and told her.

"It can't be—" she exclaimed.

I nodded, my eyes burning from the sting of tears. She

went to the kitchen window and looked out into the dawn. Silver lay like a shadow, black against the green ferns.

"Why, she's just sleeping," my mom said, not believing.

"No," I said. "She's dead. Silver's dead."

And then I walked upstairs to my room, feeling dead myself. I heard my mom go out the back door, which didn't close behind her, and then I heard my dad's voice. The door closed, and the two of them spoke softly.

I lay on my bed with my eyes shut, not wanting to speak with anyone. I wanted to be alone. But now when I closed my eyes, I saw the moonlight and the owl, the squirrel being carried away, and Silver dying. These flashed sickeningly before my mind, and I heard Max calling for Tony, and then I fell into a deep, comalike sleep.

When my eyes opened, my mom was standing in the doorway.

"Don't you think you should help your father with the burial?"

I said nothing.

It felt good in the darkness of my room, with the shades drawn. I didn't want to go out.

She stayed at the head of the stairs, and though I didn't look in that direction, I could feel her there.

"This isn't like you, dear," she said tonelessly. I rolled over and faced the wall. She said, "You love Silver. I know you do."

I hurt so badly inside, there were no words for it. No one was closer to me than Silver—not even Max. But I didn't have Silver anymore. She was gone! Just like the squirrel. I imagined, then, that if Max were here, in my place, he wouldn't be feeling sorry for himself. He wouldn't be lying down, shutting himself off from everything.

"Help your father now," I heard my mom say. Her footfalls echoed on the stairs as she retreated.

I got up, lifted the shade, and looked out the window. My dad was at the bottom of the hill, shovel in hand. He was going to bury Silver, alone. I was fighting to stay where I was, to sort it out. But there was nothing to sort, really.

My dad started digging the grave. Silver was lying under the pines where I'd left her, in the cool shade, in the very place where she liked to sleep on hot summer days.

I went downstairs and walked out into the numb afternoon.

"Can I help?" I asked.

"Do you want to?" He looked up from his shovel.

"Sure, I'll help."

I picked up a crow bar, put it under a big rock, and levered it loose. My dad got the shovel under it and dumped it. Then I went after another one.

Before long, we were both wet with sweat. The mosquitoes were taxiing around, biting us on our necks.

"Was it rabies?" I asked while we were taking a breather.

My dad wiped his forehead with a handkerchief.

"I don't know for sure." He sighed loudly. "It looks like poisoning to me."

He was a dark-faced, squarely built man in his mid-fifties.

He wasn't tall, but his shoulders were broad and his arms were very muscular. He was built like an Olympic swimmer, everybody said so.

"It's just sand from here on in," he said. "No big deal if you want to go inside."

I could feel that he was giving me an out, should I want to leave.

"I'll see it through."

My mom came down from the house with a couple of glasses of lemonade, which we each downed in one swallow. Then my dad straightened the edges of the grave, and I hand-scooped it clean. It was a big square hole.

"All right, I'll take care of the rest," he offered softly.

The whole time we'd been working, I'd made sure not to look at Silver. Now I glanced over at her, once, very quickly. She was not the same—I saw that immediately. It was okay to look; the black against the green, a perfect shadow. The word *dead* was all right now.

I remembered when we first got her, when she was a pup. She spent that night in the boathouse. I couldn't stand to hear her whimpering, so I went down the hill to comfort her. But when I came into the boathouse—there aren't any electric lights in there—I couldn't see her. I could hear her, though, the little fluffy ball of darkness. I lay down beside her and stayed with her the whole night.

Now, watching my dad lift her up and lower her into the hole, it was hard to believe she had ever been a puppy or had lived a life.

My mom called down from the house. "Jeff," she said, "it's Max."

"Go ahead," my dad said.

I wanted to say something to Silver. I wanted to tell her that I missed her and that I hoped she was all right, wherever she was, and that I'd never forget her. Instead, I walked up the hill to the house and got the phone.

"Tony's dead." Max's voice sounded unemotional. "Just like Silver. Came home an hour ago, staggering. Face all covered with foam."

"My dad says it's a poisoning," I said.

" 'Course it's a poisoning," Max exclaimed. "Who doesn't know that?" One thing about Max, he was definite. First it was definitely rabies, now definitely poisoning.

I was silent for a moment.

Max said bitterly, "You know, there's plenty of people around here that hate dogs."

"Like who?"

"Tell you tomorrow . . . " He broke off. "Gotta go."

I hung up the phone and looked out the kitchen window, wondering if there really were people around the lake who hated dogs. In the pine grove, my dad was finishing Silver's grave. I'll never see her again, I told myself. Never.

4 · Notetakers

By the next morning the news had gotten around the lake. I don't think our phone ever stopped ringing. But now it wasn't two dogs, it was more than a dozen, all dead in less than twenty-four hours. And all brought down by the same mysterious illness. On the way to the crow's nest I asked myself how many dogs would have to die before somebody would do something about it. But then I wondered, What, really, could anyone do?

A cardinal shot past me, veering toward the swamp. I trudged uphill, looking back quickly to see that bright bit of flame disappear in the tamaracks. Max was waiting for me when I got there, arms folded confidently, face fixed with a superior smile. He was Max, the hunter. The woodsman, marksman. Beside him, I felt that I, too, had some of his fearlessness. When my feet were on the top rung of the ladder, he came forward to meet me.

He dropped his news in a rush.

"They've got detectives working on it," he said smartly.

"Who said?"

"Don't you read? The *Village Gazette*. They're calling the deaths a mass poisoning!"

"Real detectives?" I asked, surprised.

"You ever hear of fake ones?" he said, his voice full of scorn.

"Well, no, but . . ."

"Look," he said, "you're no hunter unless you can smell the tracks." He eyed me critically.

"What tracks?"

"Hey, pal, use your nose. That's what it's there for."

I shrugged listlessly. I wasn't sure what he was getting at, but, as usual, it was something new.

"You sound like you know something," I said, trying to edge him back into talking easy with me.

Max turned away, walked to the edge of the crow's nest. Then, coming about face, he gave me a penetrating glance. His cinnamon eyelashes shaded his pale hunter's eyes, giving him a sleepy look.

"Could be the Jews again," he remarked secretively.

"Jews? What do they have to do with it?" I asked, startled. Of course I knew the immigrant families in Oak Wood were mostly Jews and that Max was suspicious of them. Even so I had no real idea where he was going with this.

"Plenty," he answered. He plucked a piece of sap off a pine bough and surveyed the lake thoughtfully. I went over and stood next to him. It was a beautiful summer day, a day to be alive. I thought of Silver and shivered.

"You can always tell a Jew," Max said.

"How?" I asked.

He narrowed his eyes slightly. "By the name, of course," he replied. "The last name's always a giveaway. You know, Klein, Cohen, Beinfest, Bergmaier."

I looked at the sunspots flickering like sequins on the lake. Could it be true? But how would that prove anything? A crow fell out of the sky, cawing. He seemed surprised that we were so high up in his world.

"Look," I said, "why don't we do a little detective work ourselves? Bet we could find out a lot. People will tell a kid anything."

Max nodded, spat at the hard-oak railing, hit it. Then he turned and winked. "That ain't a bad idea, Hausy," he said jokingly.

He often called me Hausy, and I called him Maxy. These names, friendly and familiar, were our way of being best friends even when we were having a disagreement about something.

"All right, Hausy. Tomorrow night, sleep over at my house."

I nodded my agreement, and he said, "We'll both keep diaries and write down everything we see and hear. You know, like when you meet someone, you ask him innocent little questions."

"Like a trap, kind of?" I suggested.

He blinked his ice-blue eyes and nodded. A thin smile slipped across his lips.

"Kind of plain questions," he replied, "aimed at finding out whether someone's guilty or not. Afterwards, write it all down. Then, when you sleep over, we'll compare notes, by flashlight."

I didn't see what he was getting at. Why so much secrecy?

"Can't we just read them the usual way?" I questioned.

Max's wary eyes moved slyly around my face, as if seeing me for the first time.

"By flashlight," he whispered. "It's the only way."

I was still wondering why, when Max turned abruptly and started down the ladder. "So, tomorrow night, Hausy."

"Tomorrow night."

I watched him go down the ladder, and when he got to the bottom he said, "Hey, I almost forgot to tell you. My dad bought me a new trap."

"What kind?" I asked as I followed him down.

"It's a Have-A-Heart. Guar-an-teed to catch anything— we'll catch some flying squirrels for sure."

He started off into the pine grove, heading for the old log-ger's road that was the shortcut to his house.

"Good-bye . . . Maxy," I said. But the name sounded strange. Sometimes he seemed neither Max nor Maxy to me, but some other person. Some stranger I hardly knew.

5 · Mixed Blood

My mom always tucked me in at night, even though she and I both knew that I was too old for this. I vowed that was one thing Max would never find out. However, since my mom didn't tuck me in when Max spent the night, how would he ever know?

Secrets.

And secret places to put them in.

I had lots of them, little pockets to put things in. Hidey holes, I called them when I was little—coffee cans full of forgotten treasures buried under the pines. Now my hidey holes, it seemed, were in my head, and the treasures I put in them were harder and harder to get at. I reached deep for the thing that was bothering me, deciding suddenly to share it with my mom.

"I heard a secret today," I told her after I'd gotten into bed.

"Oh?" she said curiously, waiting for me to go on.

I looked at her face in the light of the lamp and thought

how lovely she was, but I felt ashamed of myself for thinking this. You weren't supposed to look at your mom and think such a thing; if you did, she would stop being your mom. But I had to admit, my mom was different. She was beautiful, even other people said so, and there was something about her face. Her eyes, almond-shaped, were spaced well apart, giving her the appearance of a woodland Indian, which wasn't surprising because she had some Iroquois ancestry, as well as some Dutch, English, and Scotch thrown in. Although I was her son, I had none of her exotic looks—at least not that I could see.

"What was this secret?" she asked, tucking the top sheet tightly around me. Outside, the wind fingered the pines and made that soft music, which is the sound of the sea.

I didn't know quite how to start off. Uneasily, I asked, "Do you think the dog poisoner might be a Jewish person?"

My mom regarded me steadily and calmly. She and my dad were great at that, keeping their expressions and opinions to themselves. They were both quiet and private, but they thought deeply about things and rarely rushed into a conversation without giving it a lot of thought.

"It's what I heard, in town," I added.

"Is that so?" she said, still looking at me. Then, brushing my hair away from my forehead, she said with a sigh, "People will say anything. It doesn't mean it's true."

"What if it *is* true?"

My mom smiled. "Ah, the old 'what-if' game. Remember we used to play it when you were a little boy? You'd say,

'What if a herd of elephants was drinking up all the water in the lake, then what would we do?' "

She started to laugh.

"I don't think it's funny," I said. "I think it's sad."

"It *is* sad," she said.

Her hand on my forehead was soothing, cool. The pines at the window made a tapping sound.

"Well," she remarked seriously, "if the rumor you heard is true, then you could be as guilty as anyone."

"What's that supposed to mean?"

"It's no secret, dear. Your father's a Hungarian Jew. You know that. Both of his parents were Jewish. That makes you . . . half Jewish, doesn't it?"

"It can't mean that. I mean, it shouldn't."

Suddenly I felt hot all over. Prickly.

"Why not, dear? What's wrong with being Jewish?"

"Well, I am not really Jewish, am I?"

She patted the covers, tucking them tighter.

"Most of Oak Wood's Jewish," she explained. "You do remember we lived there for a year, don't you?"

I did remember, but just barely.

"The place is really a kibbutz," she said.

"A kibbutz?"

"Yes, a commune."

I sat up, loosening the straight-jacket sheet and coverlet.

"What's a commune, then?"

"Well," she said, "a commune is a farm where everyone helps everyone else. The planting and harvesting are shared by the community."

I'd heard of communes. But why, I wondered, were the Jews suspicious? Max thought they were; I didn't really know. Naturally, I'd known of my dad's being Jewish. But I had never really thought about what that made me. Because of my last name and my friendship with Max, I was taken for the son of a German immigrant, an Aryan and a Protestant.

"So, if I'm half Jewish," I asked, "how come I don't know anything about being a Jew? How come we've never even been to a Jewish church?"

"A synagogue," she corrected, straightening the bed again.

I continued to sit up, arms folded. "How is it Dad doesn't let on that he's Jewish? Not ever."

"Maybe he'd say that being Jewish isn't about going to temple or anything like that."

I pressed on, feeling her reluctance. "Then what is it about?"

She said gently, "It's about knowing your heritage."

"Dad never talks about that."

"He doesn't have to. He knows it, and therefore, he knows himself."

"But how?" I really wanted to know. She got up from the bed and went to the door.

"That you must learn on your own," she answered. "The same way he did."

After she turned out the light, I lay awake a long time, worrying. I decided that if Max knew about my being half Jewish, he wouldn't stick around as a friend.

It would be awfully lonely without Max. There were no other kids around the lake who were my age . . . except, perhaps . . . but did I want a Jewish friend? From Oak Wood? I thought of Nicky Loesser, who seemed, just then, so much older than I was, even though he was just my age.

I wondered . . . did I look like one of them? Like my dad's side of the family?

Listening to the wind at my window, I remembered the faded leather scrapbook my mom once showed me of her family. The one with the photographs of her ancestors. There were pressed violets, markers of blue ribbon, flattened scrolls of birchbark with poems on them, and the cracked brown photographs of another century. There was a picture in that book of Great Aunt Glad. She had told my mom that the Indians in the family were horse thieves. The English side, she said, were landholders. One of them had come over on the *Mayflower,* and his name, Thomas Little, was inscribed on Plymouth Rock.

There was the portrait of the mercenary, the pirate, whose children passed him on the wharves of New London without a word. There was the wolf hunter, Squire Little, who was eaten, one frozen winter's night, by the very pack of wolves that he'd been hunting. All these tintypes had been gathered up by my grandfather, who was something of an historian, our family historian, anyway.

But who could say if any of it were true?

The real question was, Where were the pictures of my father's family, the immigrants? The Hungarian Jews?

Where were they?

6 · Dump Dog

I awoke the next morning still wondering who I was . . . but, more importantly, one question that pushed away the others clung to my mind like the spiderwebs you walk through in the woods. And that question was: Would Max still like me if he knew? Which led to: If he knew what? And the dim echo of an answer: If he knew about me.

As planned, I went to Max's house, deciding to take the shortcut through the pine grove by the Oak Wood–Deserted Village dump. I passed through the meadow, the cave with its hanging trellis of wild chokecherry leaves. Then I walked along the old logger's road that connected the north end of the lake, which was Oak Wood, with the south end of Deserted Village, where Max lived. The road went uphill, past the ruined farmhouse, the old Hawkins place. Every time I came this way, I thought of the legends the great pines might have stored, if, in fact, trees could store anything but sap. Walking in their shadows, I remembered the three-hundred-year-old tree that lightning had brought down one year. Charlie Wyman, who owned the lumberyard, had counted the rings. "Imagine," my dad had said, "that old pine was around when George Washington danced the waltz at his inaugural ball."

My dad was always talking about history, especially American history. One time he'd said, "The greatest moment of my life was when I became an American." Walking along and looking at the dark groves of white pine, I thought about how my dad had kind of made his own personal religion of being not an outsider, a European Jew, but an insider, an American. Sometimes he would even speak the slang he'd picked up in the city, saying things like "Toid Avenue and Toidy-toid Street" because they reminded him not of his own origins, but of the city that had sheltered him.

The road twisted and turned for a mile or more, then dipped down into the sandy gully that was the Oak Wood–Deserted Village dump. From there, you could see the first houses of Deserted Village, Max's among them. The white spire of the Methodist Church stabbed the blue sky with its sentinel peak.

For a moment, I paused to look at it. I had spent years in there with my mom and had, in fact, become a member of that church. Was I—a Methodist? Could a half-Jew be a whole Methodist?

The wafers and the wine, the happy, sad, formal singing— how many years had it been since she'd made me go to church . . . three, four? My dad never went. Sundays he spent outdoors, paddling his red canoe.

And now that I'd come to the dump, I recalled another memory: how, when I was little, I believed the dump was Hell. Our minister, Mr. Freestone, spoke of Hell. And so it was that I imagined the dump was full of little blue devils. Of a summer night you could see them, dancing to the *poof* of exploding pop bottles. If this was Hell, though, I wanted to be there, and so did all the other kids in town. For the dump was a world of treasure and trash, of old player pianos, claw-foot tubs, and rampaging rats.

Now that I was grown, or almost, the dump still held the same fascination for me. Mr. Kisselbrock was there, puffing on his pipe, sitting on an old bus seat in front of his tar-paper shack. In spite of the fact that it was summer, there was always woodsmoke coming out of his jury-rigged drainpipe chimney. Getting older seemed to mean needing more heat for some—Mr. Kisselbrock, for instance. While for others— Mr. Fenster, say—winter ice was merely the frozen fountain of youth; the closer he got to it, the better he liked it.

Mr. Kisselbrock nodded to me as I came out of the brush that feathered the edge of the dump. Sitting next to him, half-hidden under a moth-eaten Army blanket, was his ever-smiling dump dog.

Well, there's one dog, I thought, who seems to have escaped the poisoner's kiss of death. And though the *Gazette* had said half the town was hit, with more dogs dying every day, old Mr. Kisselbrock's dump dog appeared to be in the best of health. Thinking of this—and missing Silver—I wondered how such an ill-fitted mutt should be allowed to live. The answer that came to me was that most dogs don't examine what they eat or drink; they just "wolf" it down, as my mom always says. Maybe Mr. Kisselbrock's dump dog, living at the dump, was trained not to eat garbage. Nor did he ever leave Mr. Kisselbrock's side. I wondered, if I'd kept Silver on a leash with me, would she still be alive? No one could answer that.

I glanced at the dump dog: he had the face of a Beagle, the legs of a hound, and the belly of a Doberman. Mr. Kisselbrock was something of the same mixture, a raggle-taggle kind of man, with a stone face that cracked when he smiled, which wasn't often. Still, underneath the mossy beard and granite eyes, he was friendly enough, if he knew you, which, of course, in my case, he did.

"Howdy," he chirped as I walked into the yard. His crooked teeth were sunk into the stem of his pipe.

"What's up, Mr. Kisselbrock?"

"No news—thank God!" he said, which was pretty much the extent of his conversation with anybody.

"No news?"

He scratched his head. Here was one man who hadn't a care in the world. Not that anyone could see, anyway.

"No news is good news," he offered. The bill of his hunting cap went up and down, and the tendons in his stringy neck flexed. He snorted half-wittedly into his pipe, and a puff of blue smoke punctuated his reply.

"No news is good news," I echoed.

This he liked. His smile crawled up, sideways, to his ear. Then he nodded, squinting into the sun, cuddling the bowl of

his pipe in his tobacco-stained hand. Mr. Kisselbrock looked
like a run-down version of some of the old folks over at Oak
Wood. But the name, as Max had said, was a dead giveaway.
Kisselbrock. Jewish, all right. And he looked—how should I
put it—sort of old-fashioned and foreign. I listened for the
thick sound of his accent as it washed over his words.

"Been out with your dog much?" I asked, trying to stir him
into conversation.

"Nope," he replied curtly, grinning his grayish teeth.

I buried my hand in the pocket of my windbreaker, feeling
the ruffled page-ends of my detective's diary. It was there,
begging to take names. And Mr. Kisselbrock was the perfect
suspect. He smelled like mothballs and woodsmoke and
dampened dog hair. I studied him as he crouched on the
broken-down bus seat that sat in front of his shack, scratching
the leather ears of his miserable dump dog. How could that
thing be alive—and Silver, my Belgian shepherd, dead?

And I thought of the lake, quiet in the sun.

I said good-bye to Mr. Kisselbrock then and followed the
dump road into the woods. Max's house was just up ahead. I
sat on a stump, took out my notebook.

I wrote one line about Mr. Kisselbrock's red hunting hat,
another about the dump dog's ears, and a final line about the
tumbledown shack.

Then a thought came to me, and I put it down:

> Kisselbrock is a Jew.
> Jews are foreign.

Dump dog is a mutt.
Mutts are common.
Nature is superior.
Nature doesn't care.

I don't know why I wrote it, but I did.

7 · Blown Glass

I arrived at Max's house feeling that I understood something. It had to do with the reason why it was all right not to care so much about things. That was why Max seemed so strong to me; he was a part of nature, cool and indifferent. Maybe he seemed cruel at times, but that was just his natural superiority showing, like the lake shining in the sun.

Max met me at the gate to his house. He had his notebook out and was waving it at me.

"Wait 'til I read you this!"

Then he grinned and said, "Beat you to the barn," and before I was ready, he sprinted off, getting a good lead. I was no match for his long legs. But I took off, running as hard as I could. I gained some ground until we reached the rosebush that circled his dad's studio, which Max called the barn.

Then, looking over his shoulder, he saw me coming on, and picked up speed. If there was one thing he couldn't handle, it was losing, especially to me. The white and black stripes in back of his Keds hammered the road, sending up spurts of red dust.

"Beat you—" He laughed, finishing easily a few yards ahead of me.

I clasped my knees, tried to get my breath.

Presently, Mr. Maeder walked up and, looking at us, remarked, "Having a little race, were you?"

He gave me a friendly pat on the shoulder.

"I won," Max said to his father.

Mr. Maeder didn't seem interested. "How nice for you," he said. Then he told me, completely ignoring Max, "After you catch your breath, maybe you'd like to visit my studio and see the glass that I am making."

He stepped through an opening in the hedge, then went into the barn. Mr. Maeder looked exactly like Max, except his hair was darker and thinner and his freckles looked more like liver spots. He walked with a noticeable limp in his right leg. And spoke with a measured voice, pronouncing his words carefully, as if they were made of glass. His eyes were the same watery blue as Max's, his skin white the way Max's was, but he was very tall and his manner was so serious that when he joked, you didn't know whether to laugh or not.

I had seen the barn only from outside and had always been curious about the sounds coming from it. Once inside the barn, I immediately felt the roar of the furnaces. Mr. Maeder was wearing a leather apron and he had on a pair of dark-lensed goggles. The heat pushed against my face and chest. But it was the noise that impressed me.

"Well, here it is," he said loudly, "my home away from home."

He showed me the first of the four large furnaces that filled the studio. All along the wall, twinkling in the glare, were crystal wineglasses. It was hard to believe that anyone could make anything so fine.

"This one's the clear tank," he told me. "It's where I melt the glass into liquid."

The furnace looked like the inside of a volcano.

"It's two thousand degrees Fahrenheit," Mr. Maeder said appreciatively.

I nodded, but I didn't know how hot that was, so I raised my hand up in front of the furnace to feel the heat coming off it. Quickly, he took my hand in his and gave it a little squeeze.

"You mustn't do that," he warned. There was a thickness in his words. "That's how you get burned. Tell him, Max."

Max looked sheepish. Mr. Maeder said sharply, "I want you to tell your friend what can happen."

Embarrassed, Max raised his pant leg. There was a creamy splotch where, having been burned, his skin was bare of freckles. I'd always wondered how he'd gotten it.

"Playing," Max said, "too close to the clear tank."

His father glanced severely at him. "Playing is dangerous, particularly around fire and glass."

He gave Max a fierce, hawklike look. Max rubbed his leg and looked uneasily at me.

Then Mr. Maeder took us to the next furnace.

"This one's called the color tank. I put crucibles of colored glass in there. Also ground glass mixed with black tin, cobalt, vanadium, silver nitrate, manganese, and red copper."

"That's a lot," I said, staring at the canisters of liquid glass.

"Here, now," he said, stepping to another furnace. "This one's got a special name. It's called the glory hole. I put the piece I'm working on in this one, and the furnace keeps it at working temperature.

"You see, it goes like this—" Mr. Maeder picked up a long tube.

"That's a blowpipe," Max remarked.

I watched as his father quickly dipped it into the color crucible in the color tank, pulled it out, and began to blow into it. He looked macabre, blowing on that pipe with those black, sinister goggles over his eyes.

However, his breath produced a bright silver sparkle at the tip of the blowpipe. The tiny starlike thing grew into a round soap bubble that seemed ready to pop. After blowing on it very hard, Mr. Maeder swung the blowpipe in the air, making a whirring sound. Then he dipped the blowpipe into the clear-tank furnace and walked with it to a long worktable.

He was humming as he held the pipe, inspecting the round bubble of shiny glass. He began rotating it, spinning it around in one hand while working a sharp knife against the glass with his other hand.

"Give me some room, boys," he ordered. "You're standing too close." Immediately, I stepped back. There was something about his voice that made simple commands urgent.

He turned his back to us.

"Too bad we can't see what he's doing," I said to Max.

"He doesn't want you to see what he's doing," Max said, looking up at the pigeons that were cooing in the eaves of the old barn.

Suddenly, Mr. Maeder turned around and faced us. He began to twirl the blowpipe like a baton. It sounded like the pines by my window when the wind passes through them.

"The shape is just right," Mr. Maeder explained.

I tried to see what he was doing, but his hands moved very quickly. First he used a couple of little wooden cups and a miniature paddle to shape the glass bubble, which was now an animal of some kind; then he took a file, dripping with water, and made some etchings on it.

"Look," Max said, "he's putting it into the annealing oven."

"What's that?"

"Don't you know anything?" Max scoffed.

"Not about glass blowing," I said.

"The annealing oven's the last furnace the glass goes into. After that, it's sort of done."

With a huge pair of pliers, Mr. Maeder put the glass object into the annealing oven and gave it a ritual bath.

"That's how he cools it off," Max said, pointing. I could see that he was both proud and slightly in awe of his father, but at the same time, I noticed that Mr. Maeder paid little attention to his son.

He removed his gloves. "There," Mr. Maeder said. "Go ahead, Jeff," he urged, "you can hold it, it's not too hot."

The glass was warm on my hand. The light glanced off it, the glass glittered.

"What is it?" I asked.

Max leaned close and said, "It looks like a squirrel, doesn't it, Dad?"

Mr. Maeder nodded mechanically. "Right, Max," he said, as if he were talking to a stranger.

As we went outside into the sunlight, Max asked to see the glass object his father had made. I opened my fist and showed it to him; it was a perfect jewel of a squirrel and, in the light, it gleamed beautifully. Quickly, Max took it out of my hand and, without warning, dropped it. The sparkling little squirrel struck a rock and broke into a thousand shards of glass.

"Sorry," Max said. He stared into the balsam trees that grew by the edge of the gorge, his face a mask.

"Your dad made that for me." My voice was weak, hollow.

"If we catch a real squirrel," he said stonily, "you'll forget about that pathetic piece of junk my father made."

8 · Gloom Gorge

Max's house was a white, three-story colonial saltbox with arbors of wild roses all around the front. The inside of the house was dark, on account of the drawn draperies. The furniture was well kept but old—heavy, upholstered, purple velvet chairs with antique lace doilies resting on the arms. There were no plants anywhere, and without Tony, there were no animals. Inside and out, the house didn't seem to be a place where any children had ever grown, or were growing, up.

Mrs. Maeder, who wore a white apron all the time, had faded blonde hair and a weary smile. She seemed tired and fretful whenever I was over there. Maybe she was always like that. In any case, Max was careful to keep out of her way.

Dinner that evening was boiled beef, new potatoes, and mountains of steaming sauerkraut. None of these I had much liking for, but I kept this a secret. Before the meal was through, I asked for a second helping, just to be polite. Max, of course, would never have done such a thing at my house. He ate like a woodsman, but only when he was hungry.

No one spoke much at Max's house. I thought of the meal-times at our place and how talkative my mom was. We all told stories, and even my dad, who was generally quiet, liked to spin a fable or two at dinner.

I watched Mrs. Maeder out of the corner of my eye. She was like an attentive bird, glancing here and there as she got up to serve us more sauerkraut and potatoes. As for her own appetite, she seemed only mildly interested, pecking nervously and swallowing.

After supper, without a word, Mr. Maeder took up a folded copy of the *Village Gazette* and began to read in the parlor, a large room full of plump, outdated furniture that smelled faintly of mildew. Max, after having an extra glass of chocolate milk, motioned that I should follow him to his room.

On the way down the corridor on the second floor, I saw the half-opened door of Mr. Maeder's study. Inside, books and pictures beckoned, but no one—except Mr. Maeder and maybe Max—ever went in there.

"Your parents don't talk much at the table," I commented when we were inside Max's room, sitting on his large double-poster bed, with the lights off.

Max grunted agreement. Flicking on his flashlight, he said, "Let's see your notebook."

I showed it to him, and he read it through in silence. I saw him come to the part about Mr. Kisselbrock and the dump dog.

He looked at me mockingly, then snapped the book shut and beamed his flashlight in my eyes.

"That's pretty corny, Hausy. You can do a lot better than that." He whirled the beam in circles on the ceiling.

"What's so bad about it?"

"It's kind of like . . . poetry," he remarked, somewhat disgusted.

"What's wrong with poetry?" I asked, but I already knew what he would say; he had no use for the stuff, there was nothing practical in it.

"A self-respecting detective would never write hogwash like this," he said disparagingly. He got up and turned on the light in the room.

I felt myself getting prickly. The one thing I could do better than Max was write. I knew it, and he knew it.

"What am I supposed to put in here?" I asked Max. My voice was a little unsteady with anger.

"A real detective makes lists," he said, "not junk that sounds like poetry."

Max's eyes flashed in the darkness, and then he sighed loudly. "Besides, Kisselbrock didn't do it—you're wasting time even talking to him."

I felt hot again. "You said we were supposed to give everyone the once-over. Don't you think with all the dogs getting poisoned, it's suspicious that Kisselbrock's dump dog is A-okay?"

Max smirked condescendingly. He tossed me his own notebook. "Here, have a look at this." He gestured, then stared up at the ceiling.

His notes were legible; his handwriting perfect. What he'd put down was a long list of names.

"What's this supposed to prove?" I wanted to know.

Max's level gaze went straight into my eyes. "Let me ask you this: Who are the most suspicious people on the lake?"

I shrugged.

Max threw his arms in the air and again stared at the ceiling, as if appealing to a higher authority.

"Think about it," he said. Then he whistled through his teeth, as I'd seen his father do. I said nothing as he raised his eyebrows and fixed me with another of his accusatory stares. "There's the Bergmaiers, the Fensters, the Blooms, the—"

"What are you talking about, Max? Just tell me!"

"Okay," he snapped. "The list you're looking at here's all Jews." He pointed to the columns of names on the left side of the page.

Mr. Kisselbrock's name was not on the list.

"And these, over here—" he pointed to the opposite page, "these are Aryan names, like yours and mine. Get the picture?"

"Aryan," I heard myself say, and then I saw with a shock that my own last name was on the Aryan roster, and it gave me a creepy feeling, somehow, to see that I'd escaped being designated a Jew. How would it feel, I wondered, to be lined up on the opposite column; to be under suspicion because of my religion?

Suddenly, a bell began to ring.

Max jumped up from the bed, ran to the window.

"We got a squirrel!" he shouted, and ran out the door.

I followed, running after him.

His mother came out of the kitchen as Max headed for the back porch.

She said, "Max, your father's napping in the parlor."

I glanced at Mr. Maeder as we passed the parlor door. He was underneath the *Village Gazette,* snoring. Even as he slept, I somehow felt Mr. Maeder's watchful eye. I followed Max out to the porch, then down the back stairs and around the back of the barn into the gloom of the gorge.

"C'mon," Max said, tugging my sleeve, "the trap's down there."

The bell was ringing now with less urgency. We went farther behind the barn, where Mr. Maeder had placed a row of black barrels. Even with the tops on, they gave off a peculiar odor. The ferns all around them were yellow and white, their natural color bleached away. I could see a metal box, partially covered with leaves, lying at the base of a great, rough-barked oak.

"That's the Have-A-Heart trap my father got me," Max said proudly. "Look, we've caught one!"

In the moonlight, which poured down like thin blue milk through the layers of leaf trees at the top of the gorge, I saw the wire trap and, within, huddled in the corner, a small sleek-furred creature. Its tail was curled around it as if for protection, and its fur looked like satin. A flying squirrel. His eyes, those huge, black, shiny marbles. They looked unreal, like cartoon eyes.

"Look at his belly," Max exclaimed. "Pure white."

And it was, too, pretty as new-fallen snow on a winter's night.

"That's how they glide," Max said, "with those skin flaps between the front and hind feet."

"It flies with those?" I questioned.

"Not really flies," Max corrected. "Glides is a better word. The big eyes are for seeing at night. Flying squirrels are nocturnal."

Here was the Max that I trusted, the Max who knew the things that I needed to know if I were to become, like him, a tracker and a hunter. In the mysterious light of the gorge, I was quite willing to forget the other Max, the one who, moments ago, was playing the great detective.

Together, we lifted the Have-A-Heart trap and headed up the trail out of the gorge. I was glad to get out of there; the smell always gave me the creeps.

"Let's take him upstairs, turn off the bedroom lights, and watch what he does in the dark."

I wondered if a captured squirrel, so shy and secretive, would do anything in our presence. It didn't seem likely, especially since it had just been deprived of its freedom.

Max's father was awake when we came in. He came out of the parlor and winked at Max as we started up the stairs.

"I told you, Max," he chuckled. "Have-A-Heart never fails."

"You were right." Max smiled. "Thanks, Dad."

I tried to visualize my dad getting excited about the capture of a squirrel, but I couldn't imagine it. He would say, "Wild creatures live in the wild, not in a cage."

Mrs. Maeder, drying her hands on a dish towel, looked at the trap wearily. To her, the squirrel was just another pesky rodent. Max took the stairs two at a time.

In the bedroom, Max turned off the lights. The thin moon of summer burned leaf patterns on the floor. I made a mental note of it and thought of writing it down—moon tracks on bare wood. Then I remembered how Max hated poetry.

He put the cage on his night table, and we got undressed and put on our pajamas. It was chilly in the house, being so near the gorge. We got under the covers.

Once in bed, I felt the nearness of the moon and the ghost trees of the gorge breathing in the summer wind. But I couldn't take my eyes off the flying squirrel, which remained in the corner of the cage, rolled into a ball, tail wrapped like a scarf around its head.

"Maybe he thinks there are owls out," Max whispered.

"Maybe he thinks we're owls," I said quietly.

The round-faced pendulum clock on Max's wall made clickety conversation.

"Maybe he's afraid of the clock."

"Naw," Max said, exhaling.

He was bored with the wait, I could tell.

"It's fun to think of what he'd look like, night-flying across the gorge," I said to Max.

"They don't fly," Max said shortly, "they glide."

His voice came from far away.

"I know," I whispered. "But can you see him gliding, in your mind, I mean?"

"I'd rather see him in real life."

The voice was fuzzy, indistinct.

"I bet an owl would have a hard time catching this one," I said.

"Uh-huh," Max said sleepily.

"He's so silky looking. Bet he flies like the wind."

"Glides," Max whispered, sounding farther and farther away.

Then Max was asleep, and I was alone in the room in the house by the haunted gorge, and though I tried to stay awake and keep my eyes on the flying squirrel, I drifted off, and dreamed.

Max was calling me.

"Yes," I replied, "I'm coming."

He was standing in the field in front of the barn, holding a brown burlap bag, which was bulging at the bottom. His father's furnaces were roaring like lions.

"We have to shoot these rats," he said.

"Where'd you get them—the dump?" I asked.

"My dad caught them in the barn. They break his wineglasses, the ones he ships to Germany. We have to kill them."

We dug a hole in the yellow grass.

Max placed the bag in the hole. I could see the bag bunch out as the creatures inside struggled to get free.

A meadowlark flew by, singing.

9 · Gypsy Wood

The following day, Max had to help his father pack wineglasses, so I left after breakfast and walked home. On the way, a fragment of the dream from the night before came back to haunt me. It was blurry, though, and it went away as soon as I tried to recall it. A light rain began to fall in the pines as I neared our house. Max always said a change in the weather was good for hunting because it drove animals in or out of their usual hiding places. I wondered what kind of weather Max would use to hunt the people on his list. Once again, I felt the shock of seeing people I knew singled out because of their last names—Bloomfeld, Klinder, Klein.

Now there was a name there that stuck in my mind—Mrs. Klein. The old woman who used to help me with my arithmetic homework. She lived in a small fieldstone house that appeared to have been made by garden midgets. Mrs. Klein, whose soft skin, brown from the sun, was set off by her braided silver hair. I never knew an old person could be so girlish. When we did figures together, she was serious. Then as soon as we were through with our lessons, she was playful, laughing again.

Suddenly I wanted Mrs. Klein off Max's list. Wasn't there a way to get her off? Wasn't there a way to get Max to quit naming names and sentencing people? What had Mrs. Klein done to anyone?

And what about me? I was so worried about what Max would do if he found out that I was a half-Jew. The thought struck me: why not tell him? But no, not yet. Wait for the right time.

After I arrived at our house, instead of going inside, I went to the dock and had a look at the lake. The cottages, hidden in the pines, looked sleepy, unawake. The·water cold, uninviting. I dipped my hand in it, feeling the chill. Oak Wood lay over the hill, just out of sight. I wondered how many people besides Mrs. Klein I knew there. And what about the place?

I remembered the old Oak Wood Public Library. As a child I'd walked there with my dad. I remembered the country lanes with stone walls, houses with roofs like hats, windows like vacant eyes, the smell of wet oak leaves and brown earth after summer rain, the old store at the end of Orchard Lane, the tapered wasp that stung me on the knee.

I remembered the Gypsy poet, that friend of my dad's, Mr. Carnavali, the librarian. For some reason his name was on the list, too. How many years had it been since we had lived over there—six?

The soft rain reminded me of the secrets buried away in

the books of that country library. Now I walked down to the boathouse and got out my dad's canoe. The rain stopped, and the sun went behind parting clouds. Somehow I knew that I needed to get to that library. I launched the canoe in the lake and paddled toward Oak Wood. The canoe moved lightly on the water, crisp ringlets spreading out with every dip of my paddle.

The Oak Wood side of the lake drew near. A loon laughed in the lily pads, and a wild duck worked its way up into the sky, using those hard deliberate wingbeats that make you wonder how ducks can fly. Then I tied my canoe to the Camp Mackinack dock and walked up the pine-needled path that went the back way to Oak Wood.

I passed the gray house of Mr. Friedman, set back in the pines. My mom once said that during deer season, she saw him gut something that did not resemble a deer so much as a man. My mom—what an imagination! She told me fifty dogs had died—the newspaper said fifteen. Whatever it was, it was too many.

Oak Wood, a one-street town, lay on either side of Orchard Lane. When we lived there, our cottage was less than a block away from the library. I remembered now, that while leafing through books, I used to hear someone practicing scales on the piano. Pages and piano keys were fused in my memory of the place.

As the rain stopped, I came out of the woods and stood on a small knoll overlooking the town. The red firehouse with the bell on top was just as I remembered it, and, beyond, the town Meeting House with the cleared field and the celebrated town garden. Communal garden, my mom had called it.

And there, shadowed by gray-barked oaks, the Oak Wood Library.

I stared at it, not believing.

The stone steps that I remembered so well were just as I'd last seen them, but the building was all but collapsed. A fire had gutted more than half the library. Burned timbers lay all about. It seemed odd that no one had bothered to clean them up or try to rebuild. Vaguely, I recalled the fire, but I had never bothered to see what it had done.

I asked myself what I was doing there.

Trying to find something.

What?

I didn't know.

Rays of sunlight pried through the fallen roof. I smelled the decay of books left out in the rain.

The charred relics of leather-bound volumes, gilt-edged, lay open, rotten to the spine. They were scattered around like broken bodies, littering the cindered floor.

I remembered the neat order, the bird's-eye maple shelves, the green carpeting, the smell of paper and ink.

Here were books visited by hard rain and snow; pages frosted and frozen, given back to the earth. Owls had roosted in the eaves and coughed up the pellets of gray flannel mice. These things—mouse bones and brown leaves and so many memories—covered the library floor and brought a sudden confusion of tears to my eyes.

I looked on in blurred amazement. What came to mind was the same thought as when Silver died: *Who would do such a thing?* It didn't look accidental.

I heard a footstep behind my back and, turning in the entryway of the old library, saw someone familiar, a face from long ago.

Mr. Carnavali. I knew him, had known him well, but was not sure that he would remember me. After all, I was just six or seven when we had lived at Oak Wood and my father had carried me on his shoulders to the library.

Mr. Carnavali had been the librarian of the town; the writer, poet, storyteller.

"So," he said, examining me from head to foot, "what have you to say for yourself?"

"I'm looking—for something," I said lamely. I didn't know what else to say.

"Hmm," he replied, "looking for something in a burned-down library?"

I nodded earnestly.

He did the same.

"All right," he said, "I can see that it is so, but perhaps this something is not a book. Perhaps it is another order of thing altogether."

He was right about that.

Mr. Carnavali wore the same old country mustache, and it drooped down like the handlebars on a racing bike. He had long white blowy hair, and the sun, coming in through the open roof, touched it and made it glisten like alpine snow.

My mom had told me that he was a Gypsy, born and bred,

but that he'd arrived in New York City from his native land, Rumania, and had worked as a longshoreman until the day he came to Oak Wood to recount—to all who would listen—his life among the wise and foolish Gypsies of middle Europe.

Oak Wood, with its kindly air and good sun and rain, was the right place for his soul, and his gift as a storyteller grew so that he became, if not famous, at least somewhat well known.

"I was once the trusted guardian of all these books," he said unhappily, "the last elected librarian. You see what a tragedy befell this place, this sad abode of books and learning?"

I looked into his face, saw the sorrow in his black eyes.

"I used to live here," I said, by way of greeting and to let him know that I was no stranger to the place.

"You lived here?" he said, surprised.

"In a brown cottage on the corner of Orchard and Evergreen. There was a spruce tree in front."

"Your name . . . ?"

"Hausman."

"Father?"

"Sidney."

"Mother?"

"Dorothy."

"Well, well." He grinned. "Welcome, my boy."

I smiled.

"So, what does the young son do in the father's absence?" Mr. Carnavali said grandly.

He made a theatrical gesture with his right hand. Then he wiped his gleaming forehead with his palm.

"I'm looking for . . . something, just as you said. I'm not sure what it is."

"The son of Sidney," he roared, his eyes full of mischief. "The son of Sidney back in the fine halls of the Oak Wood Public Library. Looking for something, not sure what, and on such a beautiful day. By the way, whoever is sure of what he is seeking need not bother to look."

"When did . . . all this . . . happen?" I asked.

He squinted, rubbing his eyes, as if to retrieve the information.

"It seems like yesterday, or even today," he answered. "Well, it could be either. But in fact, the fire happened many years ago. What does it matter? The books, all but a few, were consumed in flame."

"How did it happen, Mr. Carnavali?"

"Ah," he said, "you remember my name."

"How could I ever forget?"

"So—" he said snappily, changing the subject, "if it is a book that you want, you have come to the right man. No one knows the town's resources better than I do. And if you state your business clearly, I, Konrad Carnavali, will be at your service."

So saying, he gave me a small, courteous, silly bow.

And I remembered, then, how he used to sit under the oaks and spin his stories. There was one in particular about a country fiddler who was paid by a merchant for serenading his wife; the merchant pasted a crisp bill to the man's sweaty forehead. The moment Mr. Carnavali bowed, the story came back to me, for that is how the fiddler had accepted the note, with a bow, pretending the bill was not there, and then, if I remembered right, the wind tore it away, and he went running after it. . . .

"Is there—or was there—a book about the town of Oak Wood?"

"The town?" His face gleamed like a jack-o'-lantern.

And suddenly he dropped down on his hands and knees. "Ah, it is as I said, you have come to the right place. Follow me now, and I will acquaint you with a magical and prophetic book that tells all there is to know about our little hamlet of Oak Wood."

He paused, chuckling. "I ought to know, I wrote it myself."

I walked behind Mr. Carnavali, who was crawling around on the floor, leafing through the scattered upheaval of fire-scarred, rain-drenched books. The floor was a sea of broken volumes, all of them going, or gone, to waste. The half-roof protected some, but most were caught in the weather. He slipped through the rubble until, at last, he came to a fat book that had no cover and whose spine was all but unraveled.

"Ahh," he sighed. "I knew I would find it."

"Is that it?" I asked, incredulous.

"My first book," he said reverently. "Printed it myself."

Wetting a finger, turning a page, he sighed in deep satisfaction.

His eyes moistened as he lip-read the faded words.

"I wrote so well, then," he said wonderingly, "but, of course, I didn't know any better."

"It's true then? This is your own book?" I asked.

He turned his head toward me, smiling beneficently.

"Does the name Konrad Carnavali mean nothing?"

Then, answering his own question, he said, "Of course not—not anymore. My name is like this library, an incinerated relic, something from the burned-out past. Say, isn't that what you came for, young fellow? To hear a voice from the past?"

I nodded. He opened the book and read gloriously in the same enchanting voice that I remembered as a child; and then I knew why I was there, why I had come.

" 'Here, my friends,' " he said poetically, " 'is the place for all to hang their hats. Here, the safe, sweet earth of dreams renewed, of lives reborn. Here, the castaways find their home. Here, those who have come from afar lay down their earthly burdens to breathe the air of heavenly freedom. Here, the dream of coming and going becomes a great settling—here, in Gypsy Wood.' "

"Those are your words?" I was impressed.

"Who but a poet and philosopher could write such lovely rubbish?" he asked.

I wondered what Max would say if he could have seen me standing there, dreaming amid the ancient embers, listening to Konrad Carnavali, the crazy poet of Gypsy Wood.

"Why did you call this place Gypsy Wood?" I wanted to know.

"That's what we called it then, in the twenties. You see, wanderers came here, men and women with ideas in their heads. Not just Jews, refugees from the wars, but all kinds of seekers and finders. Those were the days, my boy. Did you know that James Cagney, the Irish actor, stayed here for a time?"

I shook my head, but I knew who he was. The bantam-rooster bad guy. I'd seen him on a thousand Saturday matinees.

"He stayed here, in Oak Wood?" I said, amazed.

"And how about the Pulitzer Prize–winning author MacKinlay Kantor? Or that tall fellow, Raymond Massey, who used to do the famous impression of Abraham Lincoln, right here in our town Meeting House? There were others, if I could remember them, plenty of others. And how about that brash young poet, Konrad Carnavali, the one who went off to Hollywood to make his name by writing filmscripts?"

He stopped short, then, for there was nowhere for him to go, and he placed the water-warped book in my hands and smiled generously. And sighed.

"That will tell you something of what it was like," he murmured, and then, touching his hand to mine, he squeezed it, and wandered through the open doorway of the burned-out library. I felt his touch pulsing on my palm long after he walked down the stone steps, crossed the road into the shade, and passed under the velvet leaves of the giant oaks.

10 · Red Canoe

That night after I got into bed, I read Mr. Carnavali's book, *Gypsy Wood*. It wasn't a novel. Or anything like
that. The book was a kind of journal of the founding of Oak
Wood, as seen through Mr. Carnavali's eyes. It was the story
of his place there, as a Gypsy. The place he described seemed
to be a kind of fairyland. Here, the dreamers could dream and
not be chastised. Here were inventors, poets, farmers, musi-
cians, singers, scientists, teachers—all living together, all
dreaming of a new world.

"Here," he wrote, "was the real New World Symphony,
the hands of harmony reaching out for a common goal: to live
and work together, in peace. And while we fashioned a para-
dise out of sweat and soil, a dark cloud rose over Europe and
it rained fire. Once again, evil stalked the earth and made
men do its bidding. But at Oak Wood, man was large and
Olympian, full of laughter and joy. Sharing was our daily
bread. Children were born who did not know fear, and there

were no newspapers at Oak Wood, and we did not speak of the war in Europe."

I read until, half-dreaming, I let go of the book and slipped off to sleep.

I was on my father's bicycle, and he and I were riding all around Oak Wood. I rode in the basket at the front of the bike, sitting cross-legged like a sage, as he pumped his legs up and down, and the smooth road raced under the thick tires of the bike.

Shadows, tiger-striped, danced under us. Shawled heads peered over hedges. Flocks of grosbeaks chittered in the chinaberry trees, and garden spiders hung on their diamond webs. We flew across Oak Wood, and the wind chased us, and we washed our faces at the town fountain, and my dad bought a half loaf of fresh bread at the country store, and we drank glasses of homemade buttermilk, which was as wonderful and clean-smelling as summer itself.

Then on through the town, the little houses winking at us as we went past, their steepled roofs of slate and their mossy roofs of cedar; and the leafy lanes growing smaller and dimmer, and the shadows darker, and the bicycle, singing of summer, finally coming to a stop.

I woke to the sound of chickadees saying *dee-dee-dee* in the pines. It was so early that my parents weren't up yet. The house was still dreaming in the gray dawn.

Without telling my mom or dad where I was going, I dressed and tiptoed out the door, ran up the hill to the crow's nest with *Gypsy Wood* tucked under my arm.

This was a new feeling for me—wanting to be with a book as much as I wanted to be with a friend. How could a book be better than a person? I climbed up to the crow's nest and met the sun. My shut eyelids turned raspberry in the early morning light. Then, sitting cross-legged, I opened the book and began to read the magical words of Konrad Carnavali:

What is the nature of Man? Is he a miracle of bones, or a proposition of mathematical precision? Early on, I knew what I was and what I was destined to be: a purveyor of truth, a soothsayer. At Oak Wood, I proclaimed this to be the case, and was not jibed and jeered at, nor was I scorned by my fellow man. I was listened to; I was asked to speak and to tell what I knew, what I had always known: that Man was decent and wholesome and, like me, trying to raise himself up and speak. A man must think well of his family, the whole of it. Therein lies the link that laid Eden to waste and split Abel from Cain.

In every line I saw Mr. Carnavali's silver mustache and his great sad eyes, and I wondered whether he, like my father, had once been a bicycle pedaler, a rider on the wind, a drinker of buttermilk.

Then my reverie was broken—abruptly.

"What's that?" Max asked coldly, coming up the wooden ladder, hand over hand.

The sudden voice startled me.

"What do you want?" I said. He had never come to the crow's nest so early before.

"Don't be touchy," he said, settling himself next to me.

He was eyeing the book. Closing the ragged covers, I felt his prying eyes.

"It's just a book, Maxy."

"Let me see that," he demanded.

I held the book tight under my arm.

Max gave me a swift glance. His right hand came forward, and he cricked his fingers in my direction, coaxing me to hand him the book.

I locked my arm, shook my head. The book was mine. It was private, a special gift from a special friend. Moreover, I had been entrusted with it. And I doubted, in all that library rubble, that there was another one like it. No, this had to be the only copy of *Gypsy Wood* left in the world.

"You know as well as I do that I could take that book away from you," Max threatened. His eyes glimmered with sparks of malice.

Then he turned from me, looked at the lake.

"Hey, Maxy," I said, trying to tame him, "how's the flying squirrel?"

He continued to look away from me, but I could feel his anger. His red-gold hair seemed, just then, to burn in the sun's glow.

Quickly, he locked his eyes with mine and, all at once, grabbed my shoulders, knocking me off balance. The book fell away, pages catching in the wind. It struck the floor of the crow's nest, and the spine separated from the binding, yellowed pages whirling into the air.

I reached out pathetically, trying to grab them, but the wind took them, page after page. And the morning was full of the flying words of *Gypsy Wood*, the printed pages flapping out across the spaces between the pines, drifting down toward the lake.

Angrily, I struck Max in the chest with my fist. He took a step backward, hit the railing, splintered it. Then he shot through the pine boughs, hands clutching for a branch to break his fall. He fell on the ground, got up, awkwardly, breathing hard.

"That was . . . a good one . . . Hausy," he muttered under his breath.

I looked back at the lake. The pages of *Gypsy Wood* were all over the sandy beach and in the water.

"You're going to get it," Max called up to me.

I looked at the water. The pages were sinking like sodden leaves. I said nothing.

I climbed down the ladder to face him. But as I touched the ground, he ran across the pine needles toward me, his face furious. I saw him slip and fall, and then I started to run. His hand caught the back pocket of my jeans. I heard the sudden tear and ran harder.

"Run, you little wimp," he shouted. "That's all you're good for anyway!"

I skidded down the switchback that led to the lake, my heart thudding in my ears like a sledgehammer. On the narrow shore, I saw my father's red canoe. Taking hold of the stern, I shoved off and floated out into the open water of the lake. Then, looking behind to see if Max was coming after me—he wasn't—I lay down in the canoe.

Staring up at the clear blue sky, I felt the tears come, burning my cheeks. I listened for Max's feet on the soft sand, but heard nothing. The ribs of the canoe were under me as I drifted, rudderless, in the silence of the lake.

Max, I guessed, had gone home. I imagined him then, stomping down the old logger's road, kicking pinecones out of his way, cursing, and hating me.

I felt dead in my heart. The sun was white and climbing. The blackbirds were chirring. The mist was rising. And yet, as I lay in the red canoe, I felt as if I were the ghost mist going toward the sun, soon to be burned away forever.

Still, I lay there, feeling the quiet lake under me, the heat of the sun on my face.

And the words came back—Mr. Carnavali's magic words, Gypsy words, Jewish words, crazy old-country words, words that, no matter what he did to the book, Max could never take away.

11 · Drowned Voice

By the time I tied up the red canoe, the sun was higher in the sky, and Max was long gone. I walked back up to the crow's nest and looked for the windblown pages of *Gypsy Wood*. They were pinned to blackberry bushes, stuck to rough-bark hickory trunks, and I could even see white squares—like windows—in the shallows.

As I walked along the beach picking up pages, I kept seeing Mr. Carnavali's face. He'd given me his book, the last copy left in the old burned-down library. And in doing so, he'd entrusted me with it, handing it to me, as if it meant nothing—and everything—to him.

After gathering up as many pages as I could, I started home. Off in the swamp, on the other side of the point, the red-winged blackbirds were making their rock-chucking noises—*krruck, krruck*—and I saw what looked like a marsh hawk dive into the reeds. It was gray-winged, white-breasted, and it dropped down sharply out of the wind.

At the top of our hill I looked out toward the swamp and saw Mr. Fenster sawing ice at the end of his dock. He looked up and, seeing me, gave a careless little toss of the hand. I waved back, went inside the house, up to my room, and tried to place the separate pages back into some kind of order.

Nothing matched.

Gradually I sank into total despair, crumpling on the bed in a pile of wet paper.

A little later my mom came into the room.

"What is all this?" she asked, looking at the wind-stolen pages of *Gypsy Wood*.

"Max and I had a fight," I told her. "This is what's left."

She raised a page and read aloud: " 'The nights at Gypsy Wood were brighter than the days because we shared our lives, swapping stories, singing songs, and reading poems.'

"Why, this is Konrad Carnavali," she said softly.

I nodded. "How did you know?"

She answered, "Well, we all read his book when we first came to Oak Wood. I remember him, the imp, full of poetry and mischief. He loved to tell stories to children—of which you were one. Do you remember him?"

I sat on the bed, resting my head in my hands.

"I met him today over at Oak Wood, and he gave me his book. It was on the floor of the library—what was left of it."

She sat down beside me.

"No one knew who it was or why they did it. But the police found the can of kerosene that set all the books ablaze. Such a dear little building, too. It's a shame to see it today,

but that's the way the town wanted it left—a permanent re-
minder of the wrong that was done. We used to take you
there, and Mr. Carnavali and your father would talk."

The library, I remembered, was like a golden comb of
honey. My mom picked up the ruffled pages, put them on her
lap, and tried to smooth them out.

"Mr. Plennis, the woodcarver, built that library," she said.
"Do you remember him? He was a sweet old man, just like
Mr. Carnavali."

I shook my head, buried my face in my pillow. I wasn't
seeing the library anymore, but the leaves of *Gypsy Wood*, the
scattered white pages falling like petals on the dark lake.

"Whatever happened to your poor book?" my mom asked.

"Max knocked it out of my hand," I told her, stifling back a
sob.

"Max?" she said, surprised.

"You don't know him," I cried bitterly. "You don't know
him at all." I was surprised to hear myself speak out against
him like that.

I got up from the bed and walked across the room to the
window that looked out on the swamp. The cattails stood up
like swords against the night sky. Then I turned and picked
up a model airplane from my dresser. I'd made it in fifth
grade. It was silly, the work of a child. Suddenly I wanted to
crush it, to hear it break in my hands. But I put it down instead. My mom's watchful eyes were on me the whole time.

"I'm sure there's a lot I'll never know about Max," she admitted, "but you, now, you're a different story." She gave me

a funny little hug and added, "I'll be right back." She went downstairs, and I heard her hunting around down there for something. Soon, she returned with a book.

"I was sure we still had one," she said.

It was a fresh-looking copy of *Gypsy Wood*. The dust jacket, which looked new, showed a mustached man doing a little jig in front of a fiddler, who was also dancing. In a circle around the two of them, were a bunch of children holding hands.

"It's beautiful," I exclaimed.

My mom said, "Does that help . . . just a little?"

Carefully, I opened the book, sniffed the dry old pages; it smelled good, like oak leaves in autumn grass.

My mom hugged me again, and this time, I hugged her back.

"Now tell me," she said, "what's wrong with Max?"

"He is prejudiced," I answered, ". . . against us."

She was folding some of my clothes, putting them in the dresser.

"Against us?" she asked.

"Jews," I said. "Max hates Jews. That's all he talks about lately."

I got into my pajamas, and she closed my top drawer and tucked me into bed.

"You know," she replied, "I think the dog scare's gotten to all of us. But you have to remember something, Jeff. Max, for all his brave ways in the woods, is just a boy."

I closed my eyes and saw the hard lines of Max's face, his

hunter's blue eyes. No, he's not just a boy at all, I wanted to say. But I said nothing. How could she understand; how could she begin to know what I knew. About Max.

About myself.

12 · Deep Water

In the morning, my dad asked me to go swimming with him. I went down to the dock and looked at the lake, which was glassy and still. Black swallows with pointed wings were dropping, scissorlike, over the calm water, skimming for insects then arcing back into the sky, where they darted to and fro, and dived again.

I followed my dad to the water's edge, dipped my hand in—it was cold and dark. I didn't like to swim where I couldn't see the bottom, which was most of the lake, it being a very deep one, going down—so they said—more than three hundred feet out beyond our dock.

My dad dived and swam along the bottom, his white body gleaming in the green water. Behind him, quicksilver bubbles boiled, burst, and then the crown of his head emerged, hair plastered flat to his forehead, making him look like a medieval monk.

"Come on in, it's not cold," he called to me.

"No thanks," I answered, thinking of the deep water, the dark eels, the cloudy bottom, the odd albino fish that probably lived down there in the murk. He swam out to where the water was over a hundred feet deep, and I wondered how he could ignore the threat of the great snapper, the old man of the swamp.

The old snapper was down there, somewhere. Waiting. Or so I imagined. His little silver eyes buried in folds of leathery flesh, looking for toes to bite off.

Hearing footsteps behind me, I turned and saw my mom come down to the dock with a Thermos of coffee and cups.

"Your father would love it if you'd go in with him," she said. "Wouldn't you like a dip?"

"It's deep out there," I said moodily.

"But you used to be such a good little swimmer."

"Still am," I said, shrugging. "I just don't feel like it."

My dad's clean strokes grew smaller as he receded from the shore, going farther and farther out toward the center of the lake.

"Isn't Dad afraid of the old man of the swamp?" I asked my mom curiously.

She wrinkled her nose and chuckled.

"Why, that old turtle wouldn't hurt anyone," she chided. "The legend tells—"

"I know the legend, Mom. I'm talking about the real turtle."

My dad was swimming back to shore, his arms rising and falling, carving the water cleanly.

"The old man of the swamp saved a girl from drowning once," my mom said. She set the coffee cups on the dock; a gauze-winged dragonfly touched a white cup and zinged away.

"I don't believe that old story's true. Why would a snapping turtle save a person? It doesn't make sense," I said skeptically.

My mom stopped pouring coffee. "Most of life doesn't make sense," she said, "not until we make sense of it, anyway."

"You said you once saw the turtle—its back was as big around as a barrel, you said—"

"So I did." She remembered. My dad came out of the water, dripping wet.

"Didn't you say you saw it once, too?" she asked me.

I closed my eyes, and it was there. That summer morning I was five, sitting in the red canoe with my dad, fishing. Something stirred over by the lily pads. Something big and dark. Then a humpbacked turtle with a spike-nosed head and tiny gemlike eyes rose up out of the muck.

"That was just a dream," I said, "not a real turtle."

"I saw it myself," my dad mentioned, rubbing his head with his towel. "It was real enough for me. I was afraid it might tip over our canoe."

"How can you swim out there, then?" I asked him.

Far off in the swamp, a loon cried. It sounded like a woman being murdered.

"Well." My dad smiled and took a sip of coffee. "I suppose

we do a lot of things that we don't really think about. We do them because we like to do them. Maybe no other reason than that. One time, when I was visiting in Newfoundland, I swam out to an iceberg. Wanted to prove to myself that I could do it."

He took another swallow of coffee. "Fool thing to do. I could've easily gotten hypothermia."

In my mind, I saw the Newfoundland iceberg rise out of the depths of the lake. It was a great glowing chunk of ice; the northern lights were flickering inside it, trapped and trying to get out.

"How cold is the water around Newfoundland?" I asked.

He looked thoughtful. "Oh, I'd say around fifty-three degrees. That summer, though, the sea was calm and growing warm, and the ice was melting off the Grand Banks."

"What about killer whales . . . and sharks?"

Laughingly, he said, "You don't think like that when you do a stunt. Later on you think about it, like we're doing now."

He sat down next to me, and my mom poured a little more coffee into his cup.

"Of course," he added, smiling, "I wouldn't do a thing like that now for a million bucks."

"Why not?"

"I don't have to pull stunts to prove that I'm a man anymore, or to remind myself that I'm alive."

"What do you have to do, then?" I asked, tossing a pebble into the water.

"You just have to live," he said simply. "In fact," he went

on, "if you really know who you are, you don't have to prove anything to anyone."

"That's easy for you to say," I said. "Everyone knows you're a swimming champion. Even Max calls you Swimmer, just like it was your name."

"I don't care what people call me. It's not important. What matters is how I feel about myself."

For the rest of the day and evening I kept hearing those words, "What matters is how I feel about myself." I thought hard about that. Because, like it or not, I did care what people called me. It was important. Feeling good about myself meant that other people thought well of me. I was always trying to please others, to prove myself—especially to Max. Always trying to make him think that I was his equal. When all I wanted was his friendship. But with Max, I guess, that wasn't enough.

That night the dream returned, the nightmare. . . .

The sky was dull gray, promising rain. Max and I were standing over the burlap bag. The bag bulged as the creatures inside tried to get out.

"I don't want to do this," I told Max.

"Of course you do," he replied. "You want to be a hunter, don't you?"

I remained silent.

"No one likes rats. . . . Don't you want to prove yourself?" he demanded.

I nodded.

"Then shoot when I tell you to—" He glared at me. "Now!"

His rifle cracked. He ejected cartridges into the air. They fell brassily against the ground, ringing. Ribbons of smoke coiled around Max's head. He kept firing, the bag kept jumping. My finger was trembling on the trigger.

13 · Gypsy Fiddle

Suddenly I was awake, sitting up in bed. The night was quiet except for the barking of a fox. Just outside my window, short barks, cold and clear.

Max! Our secret signal. During the day, we cawed like crows. At night, we barked like foxes. So I knew he was out there, somewhere. I pulled my blue jeans over my pajama bottoms, put on my windbreaker, scuttled down the stairs, and tiptoed past my parents' room. Then I went through the living room to where the deck led out to the dock and the lake.

The deck gave off a winter glare in the full summer moon. The moment I saw it, I knew what it was—Max had left me a peace offering, a small cage, in which I recognized his flying squirrel, Silky. I looked into the pine shadows, knowing that Max was gone. Then I picked up the cage and brought it into the house.

I imagined Max jogging home in the clear light. And saw again the downy swoop of the great barred owl, gold eyes fas-

tened on its target. The hairs at the back of my neck stood up;
a shiver rippled through me.

I put the cage on my bed. Silky was no longer a curled up
fern off in the corner; he was a scooting creature of slippery
moon-fur, running wildly all about, trying to get free.

I picked up the note, pinned to the cage top:

Hausy,

    I went home feeling bad about our fight—or what-
ever it was. Maybe I shouldn't have jumped you, and
maybe you shouldn't have run off. Who knows? All I
know is, my mom says I can't have Silky anymore, so I
want you to have him.

Your friend,
Maxy

P.S. Meet me tomorrow noon at the crow's nest. I
have news.

Placing the cage beside the bed, where I could watch Silky
scamper in the moonlight, I picked up *Gypsy Wood,* and read a
line or two to remind myself that if Max and I were friends
again, I had to be different; I had to remember who I really
was without trying to prove myself.

We made the long trip from Hungary, Rumania,
Austria, Russia, and Czechoslovakia. We left farms and
family and turned our faces to the faceless sea. Soon, we
said, we will again till the fertile soil, the dark, wet,
dreaming land of some other Gypsy wood.

I stopped reading, not because I wanted to, but because I had to, for I imagined that I saw the face of kindly Mrs. Klein and the white-mustached smile of Mr. Carnavali.

I stood up and walked to the mirror that hung over my dresser. Peering into it, I studied the face that was reflected there. I smiled, it smiled back. I frowned, it frowned. And as I stared, other faces appeared: an Iroquois horse thief, a British brigand, a Rotterdam bridge builder, a woolen-scarved wolf hunter, a well-bred bridegroom of Ann Warren, first daughter of the first Plymouth family to purchase land in the New World.

The faces vanished.

Then the mirror showed me the face of a twelve-year-old boy.

A Jewish boy.

Then I got into bed. The faces came swimming out of the mirror after me. I pulled the covers over my head, sliding toward the bottom of the bed, hoping the faces would go away. But they followed me there, too: round heads with yarmulkes, bearded men with flinty eyes, women with shawls and pleated skirts, children whirling, dancing around a Gypsy fiddler.

And I was one of them.

14 · Salt Lick

When I awoke there was a kingfisher at my window, his rackety voice rolling me out of sleep. I opened my eyes, saw his smart crest and dagger beak. Then, in a flash of blue feathers, he was gone.

I rubbed my eyes, and there, beside my bed, was a flying squirrel! So I hadn't dreamed it. Max really had given me his pet.

At breakfast, my mom said that I should give him pecans. She remembered that gray squirrels liked them. I took a can of nuts she was planning to use for cookies and brought it upstairs to my bedroom. The sun was getting bright, so I lowered the blinds, darkened the room.

Silky sniffed the nut, seized it, and began to crack it apart. Then he sat back on his haunches and nibbled away on it. His small paws were just like hands. He gripped the nut firmly, turning it around as if he had it on a lathe. When that nut was gone, I gave him another.

And another.

My mom came upstairs, asking, "Jeff, did you thank Max for his gift?"

I shook my head.

"Max asked me to meet him later. I'll thank him then."

I spent that whole morning watching Silky fix his nest, which was constructed of shredded leaves and toilet paper. He was so perfect looking: his belly fur whiter than milk, softer than a Persian cat. The loose flap of fur that he used for gliding looked like a poncho. I wanted to pick him up and smell him and give him a little kiss. But of course, this was out of the question. Silky was a wild creature, not a domestic one. It might be a long time before I would ever touch him.

"You know," my mom said in the kitchen, "you're lucky Silky didn't get into the poison that killed the dogs. There's an article in the paper about how the poisoner used strychnine."

"What's that?" I asked, sitting down.

"One of the worst poisons there is," my dad replied, looking up from the newspaper. "The terrible thing about it is that it affects the whole forest."

"Where is the . . . strychnine, then?" I wanted to know.

My dad said, "Maybe in a salt lick."

"But then cows would get at it," I suggested.

My dad removed his reading glasses and rubbed his eyes. "You see," he explained, "if the lick was out in the woods, the deer would get into it. After that, there's no telling. Any scavenger might prey on a deer's carcass—rats, maggots, mice, even the littlest fly."

"Dogs?" I asked.

"Especially dogs," my dad affirmed.

"We don't believe it's a good idea just yet for you to be out and around in the woods," my mom advised me from the kitchen sink.

"What about Silky?" I asked.

"Well, Silky's alive," my dad said, "which means he hasn't eaten anything poisonous. But still, I think you ought to let him go. After all, he's a wild creature, a thing of the forest, not meant to be in a cage."

I agreed with all that he said, but I couldn't bear to part with Silky so soon. Maybe in a few weeks.

"You've got to promise us that you'll be careful from now on," my dad warned.

I said, "I'll be careful."

My mom gave me a concerned look.

"Don't worry about me so much," I said.

"I do worry about you—and Max," she admitted.

"I don't think the two of you ought to be spending so much time together," my dad said. His dark eyebrows shadowed his eyes.

"Not after all that talk of his," my mom put in. I figured she must have told my dad.

"I can handle Max," I said confidently. "I know I can, now."

Before they could change their minds about letting me go

to Deserted Village, I headed up the stairs to pack my things.

By noon I was up in the crow's nest. Max came along, rifle in hand. The wind was blowing from the northeast, clouds scudding, the lake choppy.

"What's up?" he said, climbing the ladder.

"You," I said, and we both laughed.

He slung the rifle over his shoulder, then pulled himself all the way up onto the crow's nest.

"Have a look at this," he said. He handed me a piece of folded newspaper. I was certain it was the article on the dogs.

"My mom already told me about it," I said.

"Better read this for yourself," Max said seriously. His expression changed. "Hey, did you get my message last night?"

"Silky's great—I don't know how to thank you," I told him, but I gave him back the newspaper clipping without looking at it. I'd decided I wasn't going to do everything he told me to do. Not anymore. That way we'd be friends. I'd decided that I wasn't going to let him get away with any of his remarks about Jews, either.

Max looked at the lake, pitched a pinecone through a space in the trees. It spun over and out, arcing down to the water, where it plopped.

"I couldn't keep Silky. My mom's getting all scared, on account of the poisoning and all. She says even a tiny little ear-mite can get infected with strychnine and could infect any animal. She's all in a panic over it," he said, staring moodily at the gunmetal water.

Then he sat down with me, cross-legged. "How's your mom taking the news?" he questioned.

"She's not making a big deal about it," I said, hoping to change the subject.

"Well, anyway, my mom says it's going to be like the black plague," Max said severely. He went on, "That was the awful medieval disease that was spread around by rats. Which is why I brought this along—" He raised his pump-action twenty-two.

"My dad gave me these long-rifle bullets that are made for vermin, like rats. See, they have a hollow point. When you shoot them, the lead flattens out—wham!"

Eyes gleaming fiercely, he raised his twenty-two, sighted it on a pinecone lying on the ground, and squeezed off a round.

Keer-ack!

The rifle sent a trace of thin blue smoke into the air.

My mouth felt dry. The smell of that smoke sickened me. I could still taste it as it lifted on the breeze.

"Sorry about the other day," Max said contritely.

I shrugged; the smell was going away. I could breathe again.

"You're not angry at me?" he said.

I shook my head.

"You want to sleep over tonight? We'll have some real fun."

I nodded.

"Don't forget your twenty-two," he pointed out.

"I don't want to shoot any rats," I said.

"Bet you change your mind," he said darkly. "Anyway, we're going to take a ride over the gorge on my slider."

"What slider?" I asked.

"It's one of those things that mountain men use to get over

canyons and stuff. You hold on to it with your hands, and then you kind of float along on the air. It's so cool. My dad made it for me. He says it goes real fast. Tonight we'll get to try it out."

As I glanced at Max, I noticed that his reddish hair was brushed into a big wave that made him look old for his age. The freckles around his nose were dark brown from the summer sun, and they were about the only thing on his face that looked childlike. My mom was wrong, I thought, he doesn't look like a boy; he looks hard, like a man.

I watched him walk off in the direction of his house, his rifle resting on his shoulder like a soldier's.

I saw the field and the darkening sky. I looked at the brown burlap bag at our feet.

"I have to see what I'm going to kill," I told Max.

"You've seen nasty-looking rats before," he said harshly.

The bag stirred and it seemed that it was trying to crawl out of the hole.

Max pointed his pump-action twenty-two.

"When I say shoot, pour lead into the bag," he ordered.

He hesitated for a moment, his lip twitching.

"Now!" he ordered. "Shoot!"

15 · Ice Man

That evening, I took the shortcut through the swamp, and where the road came out of the trees, I saw Mr. Fenster's sagging dock. He was working, as usual, sawing up ice blocks. His saw was shooshing back and forth—a big two-man crosscut—with his pale wife at the other end, trying to keep up with him. Every once in a while, though, he stopped and squirted a can of Three-in-One on the teeth of the saw. Then, dripping oil, he worked the blade back into the ice.

Sha-shoosh, sha-shoosh.

What a life....

He saw me on the road, heading for the hemlocks on the other side of his house.

"Hey," he cried hoarsely, "h'aint you got no pants?"

Puzzled, I stopped.

I had no idea what he was talking about.

The red hunter's cap, dabbed with oil spill, bobbed like a duck's bill over his wrinkled red brow. Cackling, he pointed at my bare legs. His heavily sweatered, white-haired wife gave a gaping grin. She, too, was laughing; her voice sounded like the oily saw bearing down on that block of stubborn ice.

Then I understood the joke—I was wearing a sweatshirt and a pair of cutoff shorts, which, because of the length of my sweatshirt, were not visible. I guess it looked like I was just wearing the sweatshirt and nothing else.

I laughed to show them I got the joke, and the old man beckoned me over to where they were sawing. Cautiously, I walked along the rickety dock. The cattails were growing up through the boards. All around, the bullfrogs were booming.

"Taking the shortcut, I see," old man Fenster said, winking. His face, the color of a ripe autumn apple, had bits of blue-white beard over his chin and cheeks.

"Whar's that dog of yours?" he asked, taking out a hefty plug of Red Man, tucking it into his lower lip.

I wondered if it were possible that he hadn't heard.

The two of them lived amid the cool blue ice all summer long, blowing smoke rings with their breath. It had to do something to you, sucking in all that winter in the middle of summer. Sawing and chopping, guffawing at nothing. People said they were "woods queer," which meant woods funny, which was another way of saying crazy.

"My dog's dead," I said plainly. "Just like everybody else's."

"Couldn't take the heat, huh?"

Mr. Fenster spat into the swamp water and struck a lily pad.

"Poisoned. Just like everybody else's."

Mrs. Fenster cocked her head like a funny old hen.

"Pisened?" she said, craning her neck.

"Pisened," I said, imagining her pronunciation went quicker into her ear.

The two of them looked at each other, and both of their mouths were black holes.

"Like everybody else's, you say?" Mr. Fenster cawed.

Nodding, I said, "Half the town's up in arms over it. Don't you read the papers?"

Mrs. Fenster shook her head vehemently.

"Us and the news fell out a long time ago," she crackled.

"Yep," he confirmed. "Newspaper's a pitiful poor waste of trees, you want my opinion. Not much good for anything 'cept wrappin' ice."

"Well," I said, trying to sound older than I was, "there's a lot of bad blood over this. Name-calling and that sort of thing."

"Well, I heard through the grapevine," old man Fenster said, scratching his stubbly chin, "that some youngster's been throwing rotten eggs at the Bergmaiers up the road."

"I hadn't heard anything about that," I said.

"That's because they don't print plain facts in the papers," he said caustically.

"I best be on my way," I told him.

"Good luck to you," Mrs. Fenster said.

As I walked along the dock, I glanced into the open doors of their barn. A wintry breath came out of the dark interior, where the ice blocks were stacked up like hay bales halfway to the rafters.

I saw three deer hanging from the rafter hooks, gutted and purplish. Weightless, they hung in the icy gloom of the barn. Dead deer turning on links of chain. Deer, dangling by their hooves. Were they really deer?

They could have been anything. Sacks of grain, smoked hams. They could've even been . . .

Dogs . . .

Now I was thinking like Max, again. The next thing he would've said, though, was that the Fensters were Jewish. Maybe they were. But I knew the Fensters were just two weird old coots who made their living selling ice. In truth, they weren't that weird, except maybe to someone who didn't know them. I lived near them, and their strangeness was partly my own. But the attack on the Bergmaiers seemed so unfair. As I walked through the pine forest in the fading light, I thought about them.

They were just another old couple who lived on the edge of the lake. And yes, they too were probably Jewish.

16 · High Rider

When I met Max at his gate, it was already getting dark. The nighthawks were falling low. The sound they made, swooping, came with darkness as shadows turned into night.

Max walked up to me with something in his hand.

"What's that thing?" I asked.

"C'mon," he said, "I'll show you."

Then he strode off into the dark, his long legs scissoring across the field that fronted his house. He climbed the porch, which encircled the house, and went around back.

In the light from the kitchen windows, I could see Max's mom doing the dinner dishes. She was brushing a strand of hair out of her face with her forearm so she wouldn't get soapsuds in her eye.

Max stooped down on the porch. The thing he held in his hand looked like a model airplane.

"Is that a Stuka bomber?" I asked.

Max shook his head. Winking, he said, "It's a heck of a lot better than that. Guess again."

He put the thing behind his back, sat crouching in the half-light, smiling like a cat. "I told you this was going to be a night to remember," he said proudly.

"Is it a boomerang?"

He shook his head, still smiling.

"Well, what, then?"

Then he whipped the thing around and practically shoved it into my face. It was black and streamlined like a fighter plane and it had a checkered handgrip with the name *Rueger* engraved on it. I knew what it was, though I'd never seen one close-up before.

Leering at me, he said, "Ever seen a crossbow pistol?"

I stared blankly, shook my head.

"It's our secret weapon," he said defiantly. "Our protection against—" but he broke off and said, "Wait till you ride on the slider my dad set up for me. You won't believe how cool it is!"

He motioned toward the corner of the porch, where a wooden bar hung from a high-tension cable.

"There's pulleys on either end of it," he said with excitement. "You ride on it by holding on to the bar."

I looked down into the gorge where the pale ferns in back of the barn seemed to be dying and the leaves of the trees looked drained of color. I thought how terrible it would be to fall in there, at night, not knowing where, or how, to land.

"Let's wait until it gets good and dark," Max said. "Then it'll be really scary."

I thought it was already scary enough, but I said nothing.

Then he took me upstairs to his bedroom. We walked down the hall past his father's study. The open door revealed shelves of books. The walls with their gilt-framed photographs always intrigued me. However, there was an unspoken sense that the room was off-limits to anybody outside the family. I wondered if I would ever be permitted to go into it.

Max went into his own room, and I followed. Switching on an overhead light, he dropped the pistol on his pillow. I sat down next to it and examined the gunmetal sheen, the clean, contoured lines. The barrel looked like the nose of a shark, rushing through the water toward its prey. The wire that was the bowstring was taut, so that when you touched it, it pinged.

"Take a look at the darts," Max said from across the room, opening up a brown box. He held one out for me to see.

"Bring your twenty-two?" he asked, showing me the razory point of the dart.

"I guess I forgot it."

"You forget everything," he said, throwing the dart at his wall. It stuck in—*thunk*—with one easy throw.

"Your father better not see you do that," I cautioned.

"Not likely to happen," he answered, "unless you tell."

I offered him a weak smile and glanced away.

He sat on the bed, bouncing.

Then the muscles of his face tightened and I noticed a bluish mark just below his left eye. I had not seen it before. He caught me looking at him and said, "You've been such a disappointment to me lately, Hausy." His eyes flashed icily, then quickly changed. Smiling, he thumped me on the back. "But we're not going to let the past interfere with our fun, are we?"

"No," I said, "of course not."

He placed his hand tenderly on my shoulder.

"Never forget," he said in his conspirator's voice, "all I want to do is make you strong, Hausy."

"I *am* strong," I said, but to me my voice sounded a little shaky.

"Good," he said.

He reached over and picked up the crossbow pistol, and placed the barrel against his head.

"You want to know who suffers the most?" Max said between his teeth. He continued to hold the gun to his head. "The weak, the gutless—all those who pretend that everything's all right, that everything's just normal. They're our worst enemies. You know that, don't you?"

I shivered a little after he said that, but I don't think he noticed.

"Not me, Maxy," I spoke up, "I'm ready for anything."

"We'll see," he said, his voice softly mocking, his eyes scanning my face for weakness.

"I know how to handle myself," I said thinly.

Suddenly, Max pointed the gun at me; I jumped back. Then he threw himself on the bed, spread-eagle, and laughed.

"What a joke!" he roared.

"You're the joke," I lashed out, my fists clenched.

"Cool down, Hausy, I'm not talking about you. I'm talking about . . . them."

I didn't ask who "them" was, I just looked at him blankly. He jackknifed off the bed, swung up onto his feet.

"No time to waste," he said suddenly. "It's dark out, let's get to the wire!"

Max picked up the crossbow and headed down the stairs.

Moments later we were down on the back porch, over-looking the gorge. One bare bulb lit the mechanism of the slider, which was strung out across the open wound of the great, dark, night-crawling chasm.

"Watch how I do this, now," he ordered. "Then you can do it—that is, if you don't chicken out."

I wasn't thinking about what he was saying; I was looking down into the gorge. The discolored bark and sickly trees, the weirdly stained roots. To fall down there would mean death. A metallic smell rose from the yellowish leaves. My hands were clammy, and even though I had promised myself not to be afraid, I was.

Then Max took hold of the slider bar, climbed up on the porch siding, and, without saying another word, kicked off into the empty night air. I watched the white of his socks, which was about all that I could see of him as he arced along, feet forward. The wire sang, Max bounced up and down, and the gorge seemed darker than ever. Over the center of the gorge, about twenty-five feet out from the porch, the wire sagged, and Max came to a squealing halt.

"You gotta kick hard when you get here," he yelled. "This is the hard part."

I watched him bucketing up and down to create momentum. Then once again he began fishtailing through the night, and the wire wheedled like a hawk, and the gorge grew quiet. Seconds later he was bouncing off the cliffside, his body hanging over the chasm on the return trip, a high ride of singing speed. Max laughed as the wire whined and he floated over the black trees.

And then, with a two-footed thump, he arrived back on the porch, doubled up with laughter, his voice echoing against house and hill, trailing mysteriously in and out of the gorge, winging up like so many multiplying Maxes. I left him laughing and, standing on the porch siding, gripped the wooden bar of the slider. I gritted my teeth and prepared to hurl my body into the darkness.

A large, warm hand fell on my shoulder.

I jumped and let out a little gasp.

It was Mr. Maeder.

"Sorry to frighten you," he apologized. His breath smelled warmly of stale beer. But it was not unpleasant. Right now it was somehow comforting.

"Grip the bar tight," he confided. "Throw your feet ahead of you and let gravity do the rest."

He drew on his cigarette, and the ember grew bright in the murky light of the porch. Then he took the cigarette out of his mouth and, holding it tenderly between his forefinger and thumb, flicked it away into the gorge. I watched it fall like a shooting star, winking out in the ferns.

"Are you nervous?" he wanted to know.

His voice was husky, soft. He spoke distinctly into the dark, the trace of an accent on his words giving them a grave tone, like that of a priest.

"No. . . I mean, I guess so."

He smiled, and in the dimness, his cheeks, sunken and sallow, made him seem a bit ghoulish.

"If I can do it, you can do it!" Max said, drawing near to me.

His father whispered, "Oh, sure, Max. You can do anything." Max shrank away from his father. I looked at Mr. Maeder and saw that he understood my moment of indecision, my fear of leaving the porch.

"It is very safe," he said, his breath hazy with beer. "Relax, let go your fear."

"What's the big deal?" Max said, annoyed.

"Be quiet, Max," his father snapped.

I looked into the gorge and saw the phantom ferns, the shadow shapes in the night wind. The dark sky grumbled, threatening rain. Clouds like runaway horses galloped over the gorge. Somewhere deep in the woods the hoot of an owl came.

All at once, fear took hold of me like a flood tide, and I was swept away with it. My heart pounded. Sweat from my armpits tickled my ribs. I could feel my breath come in quick spasms.

I dared not look down. My knuckles whitened on the slider bar. Then a voice, my own, surprised me by saying aloud, "I don't . . . think . . . I want to do this."

"Don't, then," Mr. Maeder said softly at my ear.

"I know it's safe, it's just . . ." My voice, quavering, failed me.

"What's your problem?" Max echoed, sitting on the porch railing.

His father angled a finger at him, and the gesture under the porch light was like a pointed gun. Max got off the railing and drew into himself.

Taking a fresh cigarette out of his pack, Mr. Maeder tamped it on the back of his hand, put it gingerly between his lips, and lit it.

The flare of the match made a mask of his face.

The heavy arch of bone over his eyes shadowed them. His full lips, like Max's, were pursed where the cigarette dangled, white and delicate, making a thin trail of smoke. Then, drawing deeply, he exhaled into the night air, and the smoke clung to me like fog.

"Your friend's not going to try it tonight, Max," he said in an offhand, disinterested manner.

But there was a finality to the way he said it, and Max and I caught his meaning clearly. He turned and walked into the house. Briefly, the smoke from his cigarette followed him, then, as if alive, it angled away. The screen door banged shut. I stood there, not knowing what to do.

17 · Night Flight

Max's face soured as soon as his father went into the house.

"You're nothing but a damn chicken. Oh, you talked big up in my room, all right. The moment you see the wire with nothing under it, you turn into a gutless wonder." He stalked around the porch.

I wanted to walk away from him.

"All right, Hausy," he said, softening. He pointed his finger at me the way his father had done, and said, "I'm going to give you a second chance."

Then, throwing his left arm over my shoulder, he walked us toward the glass studio. I noticed that he had picked up the crossbow where he had left it on the porch, and was holding it in his right hand.

We walked toward his dad's carport under the heavy boughs of a balsam tree. I knew that Mr. Maeder had a brand-new Volkswagen, the only one in Deserted Village. The little car glinted in the darkness. It was pale blue, like Max's eyes.

He held up a set of keys. "Look," Max said. I recognized the emblem—the wolf in the castle—the Volkswagen trademark.

I hesitated.

"You don't get it, do you," Max said coolly.

"Hop in," he said, clicking open the door of the Volkswagen.

Automatically, I slipped onto the chilly Naugahyde seat. The interior of the car gave off the perfume of plastic. Max placed the key in the ignition, and the motor made a marbly noise as it started up.

I felt a rush. This was more dangerous than sailing over the gorge—this was stealing a car!

Skillfully, Max shifted into reverse. His sneakered foot regulated the clutch. He backed the Volkswagen around the driveway, braked, shifted, released the clutch. The engine sang at the touch of his foot, the little car leaping into motion.

I looked back apprehensively at the house.

"What about your father?" I asked as we started off.

"He's passed out in the parlor by now," Max said.

"And your mother?"

"Sound asleep," he snapped.

There was a curved handle on the dashboard; I got hold of it and held hard.

Max saw me.

"Once a chicken, always a chicken." He chuckled softly.

I let go of the grip and let my hands fall into my lap.

Max drove on. The twin headlight beams lit up the dark road and made the hemlocks into an arch of feathery limbs.

"Guess where this road lets out?" Max questioned.

"By Hilltop, over by the Bergmaiers'," I replied. "Why?"

"You afraid of me driving at night?"

"Not really," I lied.

The way he sat behind the wheel so easily made him look exactly like his father. It was the same posture, the same confident mastery of machines. To Max, the car was just another toy, like the slider, like the crossbow pistol lying on his lap.

We came to the place where the old bottle dump used to be, and then Max drove straight for a hundred yards or so. Then we were at the corner of Plainfield and Emerson. The Bergmaier farm. It lay ahead of us on the border of Oak Wood, the last house at the edge of the forest before you left Deserted Village. A huge sycamore hung over the farm with its assorted chicken houses. It lay dreamily before us, white-shuttered, leaf-shaded, and very still.

"Here, Hausy," he said.

He put the cold steel weapon into my hands. I touched the checkered grip with my thumb. The long barrel pressed against my knees.

I returned the crossbow to Max, placing it back on his lap. Lazily, not looking at me, he rolled down his window. Outside, the night smelled of chicken manure.

He picked up the pistol and laid it evenly on the window frame. Then, chuckling, he cocked the lever that strung the iron bow.

The dart was notched, ready to fly.

"All I have to do is lift the safety and . . . squeeze . . ." he murmured. I saw a smile steal across his wet lips. He gave me a sidelong glance and yawned.

The summer night was full of crickets. The farm drifted in the swell of their song. The cottage, slumbering under the arbor of the sycamore, was like an island.

"The front door," Max said. "Perfect target."

The night stars ticked overhead, the thousand crickets tinkered.

Max sat back quietly. I imagined him smoking a cigarette like his father.

The farm dreamed on.

I felt my heart thumping, pushing blood forcefully through my body.

"Should I shoot?" Max asked me.

In one of the chicken houses, a rooster crowed. This was followed by an even deeper silence.

"Why are you doing this?" I asked Max.

He said, "For you." Then, "They're all Jews, don't you see? You can't trust any of them."

"I'm a Jew," I said. My voice was drowned by the crash of the crickets.

Max laughed.

"You're a Jew and I'm the Führer," he said, whistling through his teeth, and laughing.

Another rooster crowed. The summer night, drawing a breath, seemed to come awake.

Max said, "Look, the Bergmaiers have all *their* chickens safe and sound. And there's not a dog left in the neighborhood to bother them. I'd say they got off pretty easy."

"You think they poisoned our dogs?" I asked, incredulous.

"Old man Bergmaier threatened Tony—to my face," Max shot back.

"You never told me that."

"I was saving it. Yeah, they're the ones, all right."

I said nothing.

"You hear me, Hausy? They're the ones."

I had nothing to say. The wind crept up and shook the three-pointed sycamore leaves. It was as if a great blanket was being shaken over our heads. The pistol still rested on the window frame.

"Are you going to chicken out again, Hausy?" Max asked. He stared at me. "You are, aren't you. . . . You're yellow." Suddenly, without thinking, I reached over and put my finger over his. Then I squeezed the trigger of the Rueger.

The gun kicked.

The dart flew.

And struck the Bergmaiers' front door.

18 · Crossbow

Back at Max's house, we undressed in the dark and got into bed. We had not said a word to each other since the dart hit the door. Both of us knew the deed was done. There was no way we could call it back or wish it away.

The bed creaked, the house settled. I could hear a barred owl asking his eerie question over and over in the gorge: *Who-who-who-are-you?* To which I had no answer.

Max turned, groaned, trying to get comfortable. He was already asleep. As usual, I lay awake. With every heartbeat, with every owl call, with every breath, I heard the dart bury itself in the Bergmaiers' door.

I felt I would hear that sound as long as I lived.

The crickets rose to my ears, singing the passing of summer. The great sycamore spread down its green blanket of leaves as the night released its breath. Then the dart soared.

Who had fired it?

Max held the crossbow.

I reached over to do—what?

To stop him?

No.

To trigger the Rueger. To prove that I was not what he said I was, a chicken. Max shifted in the bed. The barred owl hooted in the gorge. I thought of the little farm as we'd driven up to it, and my heart felt trapped, and I thought of poor Silky locked in his cage.

It took a long time for me to fall asleep.

Max strode across the grass in tall, black rubber boots, his footsteps sure and swift, his twenty-two in one hand, the brown burlap bag in the other.

He put the bag down in the grass, and I looked at him. Max picked up the bag and gestured.

"Dig a hole for these Jews," he ordered.

I remained fixed, frozen in place.

"Do you think the world will miss one little Jew?" he asked.

I didn't answer. My hands hung at my sides.

Max pumped a shell into the chamber of his rifle.

"Are you loaded?" he asked.

I nodded.

"These Jews run around at night and break my dad's wineglasses."

"You mean the rats run around at night, don't you?"

"Jews," he insisted.

Max raised his rifle, taking aim at the burlap bag.

"Now!"

I awoke, my heart drumming. The dream was over. I looked at Max. He, too, was dreaming.

"Don't," he said in his sleep. "Don't, Father."

I looked on, watching Max wrestle with his own nightmare.

"Don't," he cried.

I stared at the hunter, my brave friend, who was suddenly a frightened boy.

19 · World War

After a while Max stopped dreaming. I lay back in bed, listening to the house settle. There came, then, footsteps in the hall, beyond Max's bedroom. I heard them distinctly. A heavy-footed person walked toward the room I had always wanted to visit. The secret study.

The footsteps came near, retreated, faded. Mr. Maeder—it had to be—going downstairs. I could hear him walking away, his steps growing fainter. A moment later the screen door wheezed, banged shut. I got out of bed and went to the door. The study was open, light pouring out of it. Everything was broken now. It didn't matter what I did or didn't do. The open door was like a force that drew me into the hall, across the darkness, and into the light of that room.

The walls were loaded with books, gold-stamped hardcovers with German titles I couldn't read. There was a couch, a long rolltop desk, a Turkish carpet on the floor. I could see where Max's father paced upon it, wearing it down in one place. The rolltop desk, crammed with papers and ledgers, was open.

My eye saw it before my brain registered what it was. I kept staring at it and wondering. But it was real—a Nazi armband, a black swastika imposed upon a white circle, surrounded by blood-red cloth. On top of this was a German luger, a thin-barrelled pistol with a thick handle. I touched it and, remembering what had happened earlier, pulled my hand away.

Beside the gun was a framed photograph of Adolf Hitler. He was standing next to a shelf of glass figurines, smiling. On the bottom right-hand corner of the photograph, there was a phrase in German addressed to Hans Maederlinck.

Mr. Maeder appeared in the doorway. His clear eyes, however, seemed unaffected by my intrusion. He seated himself on the straight-backed wooden chair by the desk.

"Have you been here long?" he asked.

"I . . . couldn't sleep," I said brokenly.

He stroked his chin, nodded. Then he reached over and touched me on the shoulder.

"Go ahead," he said, "pick up the picture. Look at it."

Obediently, I took up the portrait of Adolf Hitler.

Mr. Maeder sighed, his eyes watery with memory.

"He came into my studio in Berlin," he said. "One visit only, but such an important one. I shall never forget it. The way he stood, so straight. The way he looked, so dignified. Just as you see in this picture, which appeared in all of the Berlin newspapers in thirty-seven. Well, as you can imagine, my glass studio and I were an overnight success."

Mr. Maeder rubbed his eyes, as if to erase the years. "Yes," he went on, "it was a long time ago. Things were different then." His voice vaporized into memory, and his eyes dropped to his lap. He seemed very far away, almost unreachable.

"I don't share it, of course. Not here. But it is good that you saw him. You—a good German boy." Gently, he took the photograph from my hands.

"I'm not German," I said.

He looked at me inquisitively as I walked out of the room. Moments later, the door to the secret study clicked shut, and I found my way back to bed. But it was not until the gray light of dawn that I finally fell asleep.

I stood by, rifle in hand, watching. Max pumped bullets at the bag, his twenty-two cracking like a whip.

I lifted my rifle, but it was already over. Max handed me a small spade.

"You didn't fire, did you?"

I shook my head.

Then I dug the hole he ordered me to dig. When Max's back was turned, I bent down and jerked the bag open. There were no rats, just bloody kittens.

20 · New Morning

The following morning, after I came home from Max's, I saw my dad down by the dock getting ready to swim. The red-winged blackbirds were chirring and chucking in the swamp. I could hear old Mr. Fenster chipping ice: *ker-chunk, click; ker-chunk, click*. Then silence.

I felt raw inside from the night before. When I had awakened I knew the dream was real, and what I had so successfully forgotten for so long, I now remembered.

I watched my dad as he prepared to dive. Taking a deep breath, he left the dock to cut the lake with a toe-pointed dive that barely made a sound as he entered the water.

I sat on the dock and watched my dad's slow, methodical crawl. The way he swam was so certain. He never got out of breath; he never missed a stroke. Always the same lean, clean, clockwork movement. He went through the water like a creature born to swim. I wondered if I was born to do anything other than mess things up. I was my father's son, just like Max was his father's son. So why couldn't I be like my dad?

I watched him dry himself off with the same deliberation that he put into swimming and everything else. Slow and easy, unrushed. Always certain.

"Mrs. Maeder called while you were asleep," my dad said. He draped the loose towel over his shoulders.

My heart stopped.

"Oh?" I said.

"She told us . . . everything," he said matter-of-factly.

"Everything?"

"She told us that you and Max took his father's Volkswagen out last night for a little joyride. Is that so?"

He sat down on the dock, and I did the same. I looked into the murky water, over which the summer gnats were dancing. A bank swallow, dipping down for a quick drink, skimmed the lake close to shore. Farther out, a bass broke the mirror finish, sending rings toward the dock.

Neither angry nor sad, his gaze bore into me, giving rise to last night's guilt. I knew I couldn't hide what had happened last night. Not from him.

"What else did Mrs. Maeder say?" I asked.

"Well," he said wearily, "it seems that when you went riding last night, someone saw you park underneath the sycamore tree in front of the Bergmaiers' house. Someone saw you shoot a dart through their door."

He sighed and looked away toward the other side of the lake, where the windows of a summer house had caught the sun and were flashing fire.

Again he looked at me. His eyes held a measure of pain, a mixture of doubt and determination, as if he had only recently—and after much debate with himself—finally accepted what he'd heard.

Who could have seen us?

He shook his head, and, for the first time, I saw his eyes fill with tears. A few yards out in the lake, a bluegill leaped up. Then it dropped back into a circle of silver rings. I watched these spread toward shore.

"Dad," I said, "I'll tell you what happened."

Turning away from me, he wiped his eyes.

I cleared my throat and said, "All of it."

"All right," he said softly, turning back to face me. His voice sounded far away. He continued, "You know, no matter what you do in life, things have a way of catching up to you."

I didn't quite understand what he meant. "What's going to catch up to me?" I asked.

"Yourself," he answered, glancing into my eyes, and then looking away.

Suddenly I didn't want to see him anymore. I hid my face in my hands, and the only thing that kept me from crying was willpower. Fortunately I still had some left. And looking at the lake—not at my dad's face—I told him everything. He was silent for some time afterward.

"What's going to happen now?" I asked, breaking the silence.

His voice was calm and not so far away as before. "Well, for the moment, the Bergmaiers have decided not to press charges. What they're asking is that you and Max clean out their chicken houses. If you agree to do this, they've promised not to go to the police."

I nodded, then asked, "Dad, who was it that saw us?"
He turned and started up the hill to the house.
"Who was it?" I repeated. "I have to know."
"Me," he answered.

21 · Swamp Swimmer

Cleaning out the Bergmaiers' chicken houses was the most sickening job I have ever done, or ever expect to do. I showed up, though, at nine the following morning, just as I was supposed to. Max was resting against the big spotted sycamore when I came into the yard. He greeted me coldly. I expected as much, knowing Max. My punishment—from him—was going to be worse than my disgrace at home or the cleaning of the chicken houses.

I wondered about Max's punishment at home and what his father would do to him. And I would've felt sorry for him, except that I knew he was going to find some way to even the score with me.

As we walked toward the cottage, Max said under his breath, "You're gonna get it."

"For what?" I said, turning to face him.

"You're the one who pulled the trigger," he sneered, his eyes like splinters of ice.

I walked up to the cottage, knocked on the door. Mr. Bergmaier came out of the dark interior of the house, bringing with him the ripe smell of boiled vegetables. He nodded briefly and led me around back, where the chicken houses awaited us. Mr. Bergmaier was a narrow-shouldered little man with eyes greatly magnified by the lenses of his steel-rimmed spectacles. His voice was scratchy, impersonal—not the voice I imagined he would have. As he spoke to us, his large eyes circled from Max to me and around again.

I thought he was asking an unasked question: Was it you? Or you? At any rate, he spoke no further than to give us our assignment.

There were six chicken houses, all in bad need of cleaning. The smell that lifted off them when the wind blew was so strong that it burned our nostrils and stung our eyes. "I expect you to report back to me whenever you finish one of these," Mr. Bergmaier said. "That way I'll have a chance to inspect." Glancing at Max, and then at me, he went to the toolshed and brought us shovels.

When Mr. Bergmaier came back, we each took a shovel, and I realized that neither one of us was quite ready to let go of the summer—to give up our freedom and surrender ourselves to punishing work. But what was done was done.

So we each went to a different chicken house and started to dig. There was only one way to get the stuff up, layer upon layer: you had to aim the shovel at a soft spot, drive the blade in deep, at just the right angle, and if you were lucky, the marbled green layers of chicken dung came up like old linoleum. Then there rose a stink that attacked the nose like Chinese mustard. I staggered out of the chicken house, choking. Mr. Bergmaier came to the back of the cottage, asking what was the matter.

"Can't breathe—" I gasped.

His large eyes blinked in the bright daylight.

"Guess I don't smell it anymore," he said, shrugging. "Guess that stink's just a part of my life." He sighed, and I saw that he was as old as Mr. Fenster, maybe older.

"So, what do I do now?" I asked, rubbing the sweat off my face.

"Tomorrow, you bring a bandanna," he said shortly, and disappeared into the back of the cottage. Max came out of his chicken house a half-minute later, coughing, his own face rimmed with sweat. He glared in my direction and said through tight lips, "Can't wait 'til we're through," pausing appropriately and raising his red eyebrows with a hint of malice. Then he tossed back his damp hair, snorted, and spat.

The next two chicken houses were larger and took longer to clean. The smell worsened as the day wore on. Breathing whatever was in that chicken dung—lime, I think—was like breathing ground glass.

By the end of the day, there were two huge whitish-greenish-blackish piles, almost as tall as we were. And four chicken houses shoveled, shaped up, swept clean. The dust of excrement streaked our faces and coated our eyelashes, and we seemed to have aged fifty years.

When I saw Max, I wanted to laugh.

But he shot me a nasty look, his eyes glittering.

The day, however, was done. Mr. Bergmaier inspected the chicken houses, told us we could start again the next day, and dismissed us. I watched him walk toward his cottage—leaving us to ourselves—and a feeling of cold fear entered the pit of my stomach because I knew that Max had been waiting all day to get me.

"You know," I said, trying to reason with him, "it doesn't have to be like this. . . ."

We were walking under the shade of the sycamore, coming out on Emerson Lane. I felt Max jab me in the back with his finger. We stepped out of the shade and back into the sun. He was a few steps behind me. Overhead, a flock of grackles began to quarrel in the deep-green leaves. How I wished, at that moment, to be with them and not on the ground, with Max. Once again I felt his finger poke me hard in the middle of my back.

Suddenly I bolted across the road, running for the pine woods. Max was hard on my heels, his footsteps echoing behind me. I zigged and zagged to tire him, heading toward the old cherry orchard. The branches in there were all tangled, and I had to crawl to get through them.

I scrabbled along on my belly, while Max, cursing loudly, came right up behind me. Ahead was a field of fern, and I dived for it as if it were a pond. But once again, Max was crunching right behind me. I heard a rock whistle past my ear and another ring against a trunk. A third thumped into the ferns where I crawled like a crab, keeping my head low.

"Keep running, you little Jew!" Max shouted.

So Mr. Maeder had figured it out—Max knew!

I was on my belly again, the fronds curving over my head and shoulders. But I could still hear him at my back. The smell of crushed fern came to me as I humped away on all fours, hoping for some small advantage. He bulked and balked, banging away the branches, shearing the ferns, and constantly swearing. But then, on the outskirts of the fern field, I saw the summer sun casting sparks on the lake.

If I could make it there, I was home free.

Almost.

Out of the ferns I came running, bumping into branches, whipping through the last of the woods. Up ahead was the water's edge, glinting. I ripped off my shirt, shucked off my shoes. Hobbling on one leg, I kicked off my pants. Then I tripped and fell and rolled into the cattails. When I came up, soaked, I was free of my pants.

At once, I struck into a hard crawl, pulling the weeds out of my way, kicking for deeper water. I was not out yet—still bashing through cattail muck—but in front of me the lake bottom began to drop off.

Max, having reached the shore, started throwing rocks again. One whizzed by my head, missing me by inches. I ducked underwater, surfacing as a second rock made a string of bubbles to my right. I was swimming in the swamp. I had never imagined that I would actually be in it, fearing the great turtle less than I feared my best friend.

Max went clumsily along the shore, throwing rocks. I

threaded my way through the waterweeds, rising to the surface for a breath of air, then diving down again. Eyes open, I could see the stems of the lily pads like cables in my path.

A long-jawed pickerel zoomed out of my way as I broke the surface. Max pitched a rock and he would've hit me in the head, but I swiveled around just as it glanced off my shoulder. I was streaking now, smoothly, over a sunken rowboat covered with moss. Then the deep blue yawned before my face, blurry and unreal, and there was nothing to mark my progress.

Once again, I dived down through the gloom. My lungs burned. But when I came up for air this time, I was close to the middle of the lake. Max, on the fringe of the woods, looked little and alone, shaking his fist by the shoreline.

I turned my back on him and swam toward our boathouse, imitating my father's famous two-beat crawl. I forgot everything then, putting my arms into the lift and lull of my strokes. The lake gleamed all around me. I headed for our dock, not caring that I was out in deep water—the place I'd always feared to go. My eyes shut, I imagined myself gliding like a flying squirrel, free and unafraid.

22 · *Life Saver*

My dad was waiting for me when I arrived.

"That was quite a swim," he said. I climbed out of the water, breathing hard. He waited for me to catch my breath, then: "You mind telling me what you were doing out there?"

"Coming back . . . from the Bergmaiers'."

"That's the long way around, isn't it?"

"I guess so."

"You mind telling me why you happened to swim over from the Bergmaiers' . . . in your underwear?"

He shook his head, genuinely confused.

I reached into the footlocker we kept by the dock. It reeked of mothballs, but it was always full of towels. I picked one and started to dry myself off.

"You know," my dad said as I rubbed my head, "when you were swimming out there, I could've sworn I saw someone throwing rocks at you from the shore."

A great blue heron climbed over the lake, traveling in a slow arc toward the swamp.

"That wasn't Max pitching those rocks, was it?" my dad asked.

I watched the heron settle, feet first, fanning backward with gray-blue wings.

"Max," I sighed, "right now I wish I'd never even met Max."

We watched the last of the sun set fire to the swamp, filling it with a green, coppery light. I wrapped the big beach towel around me, and my dad put his hand on my shoulder.

"If you'd like to talk, I'd like to listen," he said.

I nodded, but the truth was, I didn't feel like talking, not really. What I wanted was to recast, in my own mind, what had happened since the day that summer had begun.

First the burlap bag.

Then Silver.

Then Max.

No, it wasn't that way at all. First Max, then the other stuff.

"You know," I told my dad, "I can remember when I wanted to be just like him."

"That wasn't so long ago," he added.

He was right, too. The days had slipped by so quickly, it was hard to believe that only a few weeks before, Max had been my best friend, Silver was alive, and the summer was about to begin; a summer just like any other.

"Have you ever done something you hated yourself for?" I asked my dad.

"Hate is a strong word," he said. He rubbed his chin thoughtfully. "I've done plenty of things that I have lived to regret."

I closed my eyes, shutting out the last of the day's fiery light. But that wasn't what I was trying to shut out.

My dad said, "There's still something you want to say, isn't there? Something you're holding back."

Suddenly it spilled out in a tumble, all of it. I told him about the nightmare and how Max tried to get me to shoot the burlap bag filled with live kittens, and how I'd stood by while he shot the bag full of holes. I told him about Max's list and his hatred of Jews. I spoke into the darkness, as if it might hide me from my shame. I spoke without stopping. And then suddenly, as quickly as it had begun, it was finished, and I had nothing more to say.

When I was through and had fallen into silence, he spoke to me calm and slow, the same way he swam. His voice, soft as lakewater, had the same unhurried rhythm, a gentle lapping.

"When I was your age," he began, "I lived in a place called Hell's Kitchen in New York. There, it was the micks against the kikes. The micks were the Irish, fresh off the boat from Dublin. And we, as you know, were the kikes, from all different parts of Europe. My brother and I once climbed on top of a tenement building and dropped a brick on the head of an Irish cop. They used to wear tall metal hats, like you see in the old silent films. The brick knocked the man out, but we thought we'd killed him. I can still remember our shock when the man collapsed under that brick. Talk about something you live to regret."

He shook his head and sighed. Then, "We fought the

wops, too. And they fought the bohunks, and the bohunks
fought the spics. There was no end to who fought whom—
and these same people would've gladly broken bread with us,
if they'd only known how...."

Pushing his fingers through his hair, he suddenly smiled.
"Well, the day I dropped that brick, I found out how to be a
member of the human race. Let the world go on fighting if it
wanted to. It was time for me to do something else."

"Then one day I went to the gym and worked out. I did
this three, maybe four times a week. I became a gymnast. I
learned to swim, and swim well. I trained with a water polo
team. Those were the days with no rules; people drowned
playing water polo. I could hold my breath four minutes and
I could wrap my legs around a man and hold him down until
his face turned blue.

"Eventually, I became captain of the water polo team. But
you know, after a while it was the same old thing: kikes
against micks, and micks against wops. So I quit water polo
and became a lifeguard on Rockaway Beach.

"I don't know how many men I pulled out of the sea, but I
do remember there were times when they almost drowned
me as I was trying to save them. Sometimes I had to knock a
person out in order to save them from themselves. I saved a
lot of lives. And the whole time I was a lifeguard, I didn't
once get into a fight on the street. People would see me, even
my enemies, and let me go by. Because they never knew if,
one day, I might be called upon to save one of them."

When my dad finished talking, the lake was black, dark.

The mists of evening were coming off the water, and the swamp was thumping with frogs.

I asked my dad, "When you were growing up, did you think of yourself as a Jew?"

"What is a Jew?" he asked. "Do you know?"

"Well," I said, shrugging, "they come from Europe."

"And from all other parts of the world," he added.

I tried to think of what Max had told me.

"Jews . . . look different," I said, fumbling.

My dad shook his head. "People only look different to those who don't know them."

I tried to remember something else Max had said.

" 'Jews have names that are dead giveaways—' " I quoted.

"Such as?" my dad asked.

"Well, you know, like Bergmaier."

"Jews," he explained, "are not only a religion, a name, or a nation. They are a family, a people."

He paused, searching for the right phrase. "Sometimes," he said, "you must use the mystical instead of the logical. I don't know how else to say it, or to explain it to you. But we are like a long, sometimes lonely river that runs to the great sea, the ocean of humankind. Do you understand what I mean?"

"You sound like Mr. Carnavali," I told my dad.

He smiled. "We are of the same family, the same river."

I was silent for a while, listening to the frogs and thinking about what he had said. As we walked up the hill together, his hand stayed on my shoulder, and he spoke softly into the gathering darkness: "When I was your age, I raised the same questions you asked; and my father asked them, in his time, as well. And it doesn't matter what guilt, pain, confusion, or doubt brought you here to this asking, this questioning. What matters, Jeff, is that you've come such a long way from yesterday."

23 · Chicken Dust

The next morning the sun beat down and the chicken houses were fogged with dust. I wore a bandanna over my nose and mouth; I looked, I suppose, like a bandit. Max looked more sinister than ever, his eyes jabbing at me, though he said nothing. Once, he pointed his finger and said, all whispery and mean, "I told you. You're gonna get it."

Somehow, I didn't feel afraid of him.

"How about a race," I challenged. "Or are you afraid you'd lose?"

He grimaced, and his peach-colored eyelashes, powdered with chicken dust, made him look dull and old. But his eyes twinkled icily, and under the kerchief that half-hid his face, I thought I saw the mocking crack of a smile.

"I could never lose to you," he scoffed.

"We'll see," I said, and went back to work.

The chalky dust coated us for hours as we labored in sweating silence. The clank of Max's shovel told me that he was nearby; otherwise I worked, or seemed to work, by myself.

At noon we broke for lunch, and for the first time since morning, removed our masks. Where the kerchief had covered him, Max's face was dustless; yet the outline of the mask remained. I laughed when I saw Max—unmasked and masked at the same time. He didn't laugh, though. Sitting hunched over his lunch, he looked sharply at me, glowering.

"How about the race?" I asked.

"You name it," he answered, chewing a liverwurst sandwich and looking straight ahead.

"Okay. We swim tomorrow morning, across the lake."

He stopped chewing, turned toward me.

"Are you kidding?" he said, exasperated. "That's a half mile—one way. And in the morning, the water'll be colder than fish piss."

"So you don't want to?" I goaded him. "You must be eating more chickenshit than you're shoveling." I surprised myself by talking tough to him.

Max spat. For once, I knew I had him.

"Hey—" Mr. Bergmaier shouted in his nasal voice, "what do you think this is, a country club?"

Max said mockingly but softly, "No, a prison camp."

Mr. Bergmaier walked over to us. Surprisingly, he went up to Max and said, "Young man, do you think I am afraid of you?"

Although he had always appeared small, he now seemed to grow in stature, to become, in some way, a presence greater than himself. He leaned in Max's direction, locking eyes with him, and, for once, I saw Max appear to cower, and look away.

Max now seemed, for all the world, like a puff-lipped, pouty kid covered from head to toe with the dust of a thousand chickens. He shrank from my sight as the hunter-hero; he appeared gangly and ill at ease.

Then, as if this had occurred to him at the same time it had to me, Max rose up to do battle. He got to his feet slowly, awkwardly. And using his height to full advantage, spoke down to Mr. Bergmaier. "I know," he said huskily, "who poisoned all the dogs."

He gave me a wink that linked me in the conspiracy, but Mr. Bergmaier paid it no mind. Nor did he give an inch, though Max's shadow overlaid him. "So." Mr. Bergmaier snorted. "You've found a scapegoat, have you? Well, do tell. . . ." He continued to look Max in the eye, his head cocked, his face a mixture of contempt and curiosity.

Max, the freckle-faced boy, loomed over him. I noticed that his head was just a little large for his lank frame, lending him an unsteadiness. Mr. Bergmaier, on the other hand, was rooted to the ground, unafraid. He stepped forward, moving closer to Max.

"We know who is poisoning the woods," Mr. Bergmaier said. "But most people around here are afraid to say anything. Those barrels in back of your father's barn, the ones he dumps into the gorge, they're full of some kind of acid, aren't they?"

Max, taking a step backward, kept up his guard. But his eyes, his most dependable weapon, stared aimlessly into the trees. The best he could do, it seemed, was pretend he wasn't listening.

"Your father dumps those barrels, doesn't he?" Mr. Bergmaier repeated.

Still Max did not reply.

Mr. Bergmaier shook his head in disgust. "What am I telling you for? You're just a boy. I'll tell the selectmen about your father's unlicensed glass business and those barrels at the next town meeting, and your father'll have some explaining to do."

Max threw down the shovel. His face went red.

"I'm leaving," he said hotly. "I don't have to listen to this." Then, so as not to lose face entirely, he pointed his chin at Mr. Bergmaier and said, "Who's going to stop me?"

It was his last defiant gesture.

Mr. Bergmaier shrugged and laughed.

"You're free to leave," he said pleasantly.

Max stalked off, kicking the shovel where it had fallen in the grass.

"Well, that's that," Mr. Bergmaier said to me as we watched Max stomp toward the road. Then, giving me a thorough appraisal, he tapped me on the shoulder, saying: "You're free to leave as well. You've done your work."

I shifted from one foot to the other. He bent down to pick up Max's shovel. I wanted to tell him something, but he spoke first.

"Somehow, I think you got shanghaied into this," he said.

"Maybe so. But I'm just as guilty as he is—more so, I'm afraid."

"You don't have the meanness, son," Mr. Bergmaier said. "Now that Max, he's got plenty of nastiness to go around—more than enough for the two of you...."

"He was my best friend," I answered.

He said, "Well, your best friend can become your worst enemy if you're not careful."

"How?" I asked.

"Only a best friend knows your worst secret—who else could possibly know it?" He blinked his large eyes.

"Thanks," I said.

"For what?"

I raised my shoulders, dropped them. "For understanding."

"Well, if you forget everything else I've said, which you probably will..." Mr. Bergmaier chuckled. "At least remember this: A coward always sweats in the water."

Then he patted me on the back and walked away, and I returned to sweeping up the last chicken house. I finished, first my leftover work, then Max's. Somehow I didn't mind it. In fact, I almost—but not quite—liked it. Because for the first time in weeks, maybe months, I felt really free.

Also, for the first time, I thought I understood something about the deaths of all those dogs. Nobody knew. That's why they were pointing fingers. Mr. Bergmaier didn't know any more than anyone else did. I guess it was just as my dad had said, "Let the world go on fighting, if it wanted to. It was time for me to do something else."

On the way home, I expected to see Max waiting for me across the road. But he wasn't there. Nor was he hanging out by the cutoff, where the old logger's path crosses the hill and leads to the lake.

As I walked under the crow's nest, I was sure I saw him, looking down in that lordly way of his, motioning at me with his chin. But he wasn't there, just in my mind.

He wasn't anywhere I thought he'd be.

He was home, I decided, waiting for tomorrow morning.

24 · Turtle Back

I arose at dawn. Silky was awake, cracking a nut. I gave her my usual greeting—a squeak—and noticed a stirring in the toilet-paper castle she'd made into a nest. Amid the lacy chewings, there were three little shrimps. Looking closer, I realized those shrimps were baby flying squirrels. Amazing—Silky was a mom! I pressed my face to the cage; they were so small, I could've put all of them in a teaspoon. Hard to believe this great gift had come from Max—whom I was now to meet in a fearsome contest. Thinking of that, my heart jumped. I said good-bye to Silky, promising myself that when her babies got bigger, I'd let the whole family go free in the woods.

I went down to the kitchen and picked up a can of Crisco cooking fat. My dad claimed it helped him keep warm when he went swimming in the spring before the ice was off the lake. I thought I'd give it a try. It was like white axle grease, but I rubbed it all over. Then I put on an old pair of jeans, a beat-up sweatshirt, and went outside. The air was autumn crisp, the way it is sometimes on the lake in summer.

I walked up the hill to the crow's nest. He was there, waiting. His father was there, too. Max wore a Shetland wool sweater and a pair of sweatpants. He nodded to me stonily, his face grimly set for the race. His father appeared more remote, standing apart from each of us, even his son.

We walked silently down the hundred pine-block steps my grandfather had carved out of the hill in the thirties. The sky was gray, ominous. A storm settling on the swamp. Dark clouds moved across the sky, and the lake lay like a bowl of cool green Jell-O. Not a boat to be seen. The mist rising, tangling, and untangling in the cloud-covered sun.

Some crows went by, skirting us, dropping into the pines, raising a racket of protest. In the woods, somewhere back where the old logger's road ran into the meadow, a red-eyed vireo began to sing a spiral song.

I wished, then, that I were loafing somewhere with Silver, sitting on a log, throwing sticks, or just out walking, looking for red efts and owl nests....

Max got out of his clothes hurriedly. I wondered if he were as scared as I was... my hands shaking—partly from the cold. He stood then, arms folded, skin goose-bumped in the sunless dawn. Waiting.

When we both were in our bathing trunks, I reached out my hand and said, "Good luck."

Max turned from me, left me standing there, hand in the air. Mr. Maeder said, "Max, be a sport, now ..." but he paid no attention. His face, overcast like the morning sky, gave no hint we'd ever been friends.

"Good luck," I said again, as much to myself as to Max.

And then we went into the water—a million needlepoints jabbing into my skin. . . .

So much for Crisco.

The cold burn of the water bit my groin, then creep-crawled higher up as I went deeper in. My skin felt as if I'd been given a rubdown with crushed glass.

When it was at my armpits, I began to feel numb.

Max, acting tough, quickly took the lead, thrashing out ahead of me.

I let him take it. Reach and pull, reach and pull, measuring and martialing, not worrying about anything, but always keeping on—that was the way my dad did it. And so would I.

Max was soon way ahead of me. All I saw of him were his feet flutter-kicking in the froth made by the blind momentum of his arms.

That will tire you, I thought. Better not rush out; better hold back.

And the gabbing crows returned, bickering in circles over us, dipping down, cawing at us, then splintering into twos and heading across the lake, growing smaller—black midnight feathers—and gone.

A cramp caught me in the belly. I eased into it and it relaxed a little. But it spasmed as I swam along. I ignored it, and after a while it went away.

Mustn't think of cramping—mustn't think of anything except swimming. I took in a swallow of lakewater. Spat some out. Choked. I stopped and began to tread water. Max was way out, holding his lead. I could hear him choffing through the windy waves.

The weather turned foul. A spattering rain came, wind-driven, building into hard, bullet drops, coming down like rifleshot.

I looked for Max, but couldn't make him out.

A flash of lightning crackled across the gray sky. Spray struck my face. Heavy as anchors, my legs kicked on. I was still unable to see Max, because of the dancing raindrops rattling all around me as the storm began to pick up.

Now the waves lifted and pounced, catlike. I turned over and did the backstroke; changed neither direction nor rhythm, but saved my strength by putting my back into it. The clouds came down, and the water went up in cones of spray to meet them. Between the worlds of lake and sky, there was no margin, no line of shore. The rising water was growing more dangerous every minute.

The need to rest came sooner than I wanted it to. The waves were rolling over the back of my head. They seemed to be playing with me—no longer catty, but angry, like rough sporting seals. I was tugged under. I came up, spitting and coughing. Somewhere nearby, Max was yelling.

Where was I? And where was he?

Wind ripped at the lake, hitting fore and aft, side to side. For the first time, I thought I might be drowning.

Then I heard Max, ahead of me, somewhere near.

Calling out for help.

Thunder boomed.

"Where are you?" I yelled.

Nothing.

The choppy water was settling into gloomy swells, pitching me up and down like a cork. Suddenly I saw him in front of me, floundering. He was ten feet away. A mad scatter of lightning was followed by grumbling thunder. Then the lake, like a whirlpool I'd dreamed up, was dragging me down—and it was real, not imagined. I saw Max in a turbulence of whirling water. Struggling to get closer, I swung at his hand, tried to grab it—missed.

Grabbed again; missed again.

That pale, frightened face was in front of my own, reflecting my own fear. Again I pulled toward him, and a wave yanked us apart. I took in some water—a big swallow. Choking fitfully, I watched Max submerge. Suddenly his head was up. His arms were whacking at me. He'd stopped swimming, he was fighting for his life; and I for mine. For a moment we slopped about in a water dance, twirling helplessly while the sucking lake pulled at our heels.

Then a big blustery wave knocked me into Max. He hugged me hard. As the water rose over us, he climbed onto my shoulders. I went down, and he clung to me desperately.

In a flash I remembered what my dad had done when people were drowning: he had knocked them out and then hauled them in.

Now when I came up, I knew what to do. I struck Max,

who was pawing at me, on the chin. The small arc made by
my fist connected with his jaw. Bone met bone; his head
sagged. He went slack, and I reached across his chest. I turned
him around and began back-stroking for shore.

My head was mostly underwater as I struggled to keep the
two of us afloat. Although he was much too heavy for me, I
refused to give him up. The wind had stopped screaming.
The storm was gusting down the lake toward Gibson's
Grove.

My legs were rubbery. I kept kicking, but weakly. My face
went under again. The lake seemed to be swallowing me. My
heart was lub-lubbing. Everything was all watery and out of
control. But yet some part of me wouldn't quit, and the
heavier Max got, the more I hugged him to me and kept
fighting to hold him up.

So this is what drowning is—a stubbornness, a knowing
that strength isn't there, that death is. A voice saying: "Re-
lease Max, give him up, save yourself." And another voice
answering "Not yet, not yet ... "

Then all at once, my legs stopped churning. It happened so
quickly: I had no more to give. Letting go, my feet wheeled
under me as if they expected the bottom of the lake to rise
out of nowhere and catch them up.

And then, that very thing happened.

Out of the corner of my eye, I saw the head of the turtle. I
was too dazed, too near-drowned to know.

The mossy bottom came up to meet me, a great round
humpback filling the space beneath my feet. My eyes closed,

I started to sink, but was buoyed up miraculously. The bottom did rise up, and I felt myself being taken away, being borne to safety.

The mist cleared, my eyes fluttered open. I was lying flat out on the ribbed floor of the red canoe. My dad, paddling powerfully, carrying me to shore.

"Where's Max?"

"Next to you," my dad answered.

Turning, I saw that he, too, was stretched out—alive! Both of us alive . . .

"He's all right?"

"Thanks to God, you're both all right," my dad said. Then, "What were you doing out there in that storm?"

"Max and I . . . were having a race. . . ."

"To see who could drown first?"

I looked at my dad's face just as we came aground, the prow of the canoe crunching the welcoming sand.

Immediately, Mr. Maeder appeared and helped his son out of the canoe. Max, stumbling limply, fell into the arms of his father.

Mr. Maeder hugged him. His watery blue eyes now watered with tears.

My dad lifted me out of the red canoe. I stared dumbly at the lake. It didn't seem so far to the other side.

"What was that . . . out there?" I asked my dad.

"What was what?" he returned, emptying water out of the canoe with a rusted coffee can.

"It felt . . ." I fumbled for the right words. "It was like the bottom came up; you know, like the old man of the swamp."

My dad put his arms around me, drawing me up against his broad chest. "What a crazy, foolish, brave thing you did out there," he said, his voice trailing with emotion.

Mr. Maeder, holding Max, broken-voiced, said, "You saved my son's life.

"I saw it all . . . from the crow's nest . . ." he said, facing my dad. "Your son . . . risked his life to save my Max."

And he stood there shaking his head, his eyes filling with tears.

Max coughed, spat, slumped to his knees. Then a perfect bright arc of water spouted out of his mouth. It looked like he'd been saving it up for just this moment.

"He'll be okay now," my dad said. "That looked like all of it."

Max looked at me, his faded eyes trying to say something that they had never tried to say before.

Weakly, he offered me his hand.

I took it.

"You won," he said.

Then, the word I'll never forget.

"Swimmer," he whispered, as if that were my name.